Rough Rhythm

Also from Tessa Bailey

Rough Rhythm

A Made In Jersey Novella

By Tessa Bailey

1001 Dark Nights

EVIL EYE

CONCEPTS

Rough Rhythm
A Made In Jersey Novella
By Tessa Bailey

1001 Dark Nights

Copyright 2016 Tessa Bailey
ISBN: 978-1-940887-98-2

Foreword: Copyright 2014 M. J. Rose

Published by Evil Eye Concepts, Incorporated

Acknowledgments

Thank you to Liz Berry, M.J. Rose, Jillian Stein and the rest of the magical team behind 1001 Dark Nights. What a freeing experience this was for me as a writer. Your encouragement and excitement is contagious.

Thank you, as always, to my husband, Patrick, and daughter, Mackenzie, who support me every single day and love me through the ups and downs.

Thank to my agent, Laura Bradford, for being a steady presence and also the first person to ask, are you *sure* you want to add *more* books to your schedule?

Thank you to Stephanie Lapensee at Inkslinger for reading this book, loving it, and giving me a boost of confidence when needed.

Thank you to Eagle at Aquila Editing for beta reading this book and wanting to know more about James and Lita's first night together—I think it made a difference to the story.

One Thousand And One Dark Nights

Once upon a time, in the future…

*I was a student fascinated with stories and learning.
I studied philosophy, poetry, history, the occult, and
the art and science of love and magic. I had a vast
library at my father's home and collected thousands
of volumes of fantastic tales.*

*I learned all about ancient races and bygone
times. About myths and legends and dreams of all
people through the millennium. And the more I read
the stronger my imagination grew until I discovered
that I was able to travel into the stories... to actually
become part of them.*

*I wish I could say that I listened to my teacher
and respected my gift, as I ought to have. If I had, I
would not be telling you this tale now.
But I was foolhardy and confused, showing off
with bravery.*

*One afternoon, curious about the myth of the
Arabian Nights, I traveled back to ancient Persia to
see for myself if it was true that every day Shahryar
(Persian: شهریار, "king") married a new virgin, and then
sent yesterday's wife to be beheaded. It was written
and I had read, that by the time he met Scheherazade,
the vizier's daughter, he'd killed one thousand
women.*

Something went wrong with my efforts. I arrived in the midst of the story and somehow exchanged places with Scheherazade — a phenomena that had never occurred before and that still to this day, I cannot explain.

Now I am trapped in that ancient past. I have taken on Scheherazade's life and the only way I can protect myself and stay alive is to do what she did to protect herself and stay alive.

Every night the King calls for me and listens as I spin tales. And when the evening ends and dawn breaks, I stop at a point that leaves him breathless and yearning for more. And so the King spares my life for one more day, so that he might hear the rest of my dark tale.

As soon as I finish a story... I begin a new one... like the one that you, dear reader, have before you now.

Prologue

God help the woman he took home tonight.

James Brandon stared down the bar, pegging each customer as they entered his field of vision. Recent divorcée making up for lost time. A new employee showing off to his blasé coworkers by buying a round of tequila shots. Two women pretending to be indecisive over their beverage order, when really they were just waiting for someone to send them drinks. It wouldn't be him. Christ, he hated this meat market. What the hell had he been thinking coming here?

Something new. *Anything* new. Lately, a voice had been chanting those words at the back of his skull. Louder, *louder.* He thought he'd found the solution to his restlessness this afternoon upon quitting his job as corporate council for a multimillion-dollar investment firm. But, no. It hadn't. While it might have eased his ceaseless irritation knowing he wouldn't be responsible for babysitting a bunch of pampered thieves in Armani suits come tomorrow morning, there was still a gnawing in his gut. A need to…*wake up.*

Fully aware that another pointless one-night stand couldn't satisfy his growing hunger for a high he couldn't name, here he was nonetheless. On his third whiskey in a place he could only describe as *obvious,* nursing hope so futile, he might as well ask for the check. But…maybe this time. Maybe tonight he would walk away satisfied from an encounter. Fulfilled even to the smallest degree.

A romantic or idealistic person might suggest James was searching for an emotional connection at the ripe old age of thirty-one. Someone he wanted to discuss current affairs with over bagels the morning after. Not so. He quite enjoyed his solitude, thank you very much. No, it was what took place between the sheets with a woman that left him hollow, and it was through no fault of theirs. This was *his*. He had a problem. And that same voice that chanted for him to chase an unnamable peak...had begun to project images. Rough, graphic images that shouldn't turn him on. But did.

Hell yes, they did.

So he'd resisted. When you came from a background like his, you fought off any similarities at all costs. His determination was waning, however. Growing weaker by the second. Making a mockery of his will.

That's when he saw the girl.

James's lungs evacuated all air, deflating him like a cheap balloon.

And in a split second, nothing else mattered but her.

Too young. But somehow he knew that wouldn't stop him. Nothing would. His body responded beneath the bar, his hands gripping the wood to steady himself. It was more than the usual stirring of attraction. Far, far more. A moving picture flashed in his mind, the girl nodding as he spoke softly to her, that delicate chin pinched between his fingers. As if there were perfect understanding between them. Not right now, though. Now, she looked lost, an anomaly among an otherwise seamless pattern of overconfidence. A pattern he hated, needed to remove her from. Now. Urgency took him over, making him feel almost delirious.

Even the girl's adrift expression couldn't hide the sharp intelligence behind her wide eyes, couldn't hide an unknown mission there. An unmistakable surety that she was looking for *him* wouldn't go away. *She* was the reason he'd come here tonight instead of going home, which had been his initial plan.

Thank God he hadn't.

When the girl stopped and faced a group of men, James rose to his feet, poison ivy climbing the back of his neck. Spiked and dangerous. Its leaves extended and curled tight. Scared. She was scared. Why? He was coming. She just had to hold on a second.

James's world tilted right along with the girl when she pitched to the side, her beautiful eyes gone glassy with fear. He moved.

* * * *

Lita Regina wasn't a prostitute. That's not what tonight was about.

She just needed to get off the street for one night. One. Night.

Thought you were made of sterner stuff, didn't you? Well it turned out, a week of being homeless on the streets of Los Angeles was about all Lita could withstand. While crashing in shelters might have been an upgrade from the situation from which she'd split, cozying up in some rich guy's hotel room sounded even better. Women had one-night stands all the time, didn't they? Dressed up, put on expensive perfume and suffered through forced conversation just to feel needed by someone?

As Lita saw it, her reasons for cruising for a man ranked slightly higher on the survival scale. She'd stretched the fifty dollars she'd vamoosed with by sticking to street vendors and the McDonald's dollar menu, but someone in the shelter had pocketed her last ten two nights ago as she slept, leaving her broke as a joke. And speaking of jokes, hunger pains were *not* one. Lita nearly staggered under the intensity of them as she crossed the crowded hotel bar on Wilshire Boulevard, looking for—

Who? A man with a thing for scrawny chicks with fading bruises? Gazes followed her as she circled the bar, customers probably wondering who the hell had let her into the swank establishment. If they knew she'd ducked in behind two tall blondes while the bouncer checked their identification, outrage would abound. How dare this imposter breach the inner sanctum?

Lita's chin went up with that last thought. She wasn't the imposter. *They* were. The privileged corporate slaves she'd laughed about with her bandmates, back when she'd had a band. Back when she'd had people who cared. If she hadn't chosen a man over those friends, they might still be there, too. Then she wouldn't be in the Beverly Wilshire trolling for someone who'd let her share his clean, fluffy hotel bed for the night. Maybe let her take a shower and share a plate of French fries.

At the thought of salty, savory goodness, Lita's stomach rumbled loud enough to draw the attention of a group of men. Men in ties. Men that didn't live in her world. Still, she sent them an inviting smile, praying her sparkly, thrift shop miniskirt looked better in the near dark than it had on the rack.

The words, *please, I'm hungry*, were burning on her tongue, but she couldn't just *say* that, could she? They would alert security or turn their backs, muttering about the lack of decent drinking establishments for professionals such as themselves. Before they finished their drinks, she would be an afterthought.

One of the men—he wore a blue button-down shirt and ruby red tie—checked her legs out, his expression relaying interest. He nudged his friend with an elbow and Lita stood there, stomach twisting, as the four of them looked her up and down. A polar blast swept over her skin, far cooler than the air conditioning. No. This wasn't what she'd envisioned, but could see now that she'd been wearing rose-colored glasses, even after being chewed up and spit out on the curb of life. After everything, she was still naïve. Still an optimist.

How fucking sad.

"How much for all of us?" Ruby Red Tie asked before tossing back the contents of his rocks glass. "At the same time."

For the first time that day, an empty stomach was a blessing because Lita would have lost the contents right there on the men's shiny loafers. They'd categorized her as a working girl in under ten seconds. Everyone in the room probably had. Maybe they were right. Even if she found a way off the street tonight, what about tomorrow? Would she keep doing this? Lita's attention spanned the room in quick jerks, taking in the way other women were dressed. How men looked at *them*. With respect. One week. It had only taken one week for her to fall this far.

She had to get out of there—figure out a different way to eat. Anything was better than being judged. Laughed at.

Lita spun on a heel—too fast. She'd moved too fast. The room spun and blurred around her, stomach clenching around nothing. Her hip rammed into a table, upsetting drinks on a pair of female customers. She tried to mumble an apology, but her legs chose that moment to stop supporting her. Down she went, like a sack of wet laundry. Down…down…

Powerful arms caught her around the middle just before she hit the floor.

Chapter One

Four Years Later

This time she would finally crack him.

Ignoring stares from her cellmates, Lita jogged in place, preparing for the confrontation with James, her band manager. This was her ritual before shows, too. It loosened the limbs, shook out the demons. She took her role as drummer for Old News seriously, same way she considered riling up James a form of art. For four freaking years, they'd been repeating this song and dance—and Lita was over it. Today was the day James lost his cool. The way he'd lost it the night they met.

Remembering the state she'd been in when James found her, Lita jogged a little faster. At twenty-three, she wasn't that scrawny, starving girl now. Not in *most* ways, anyway. The memory of what took place that night still had the ability to steal her breath, make her restless. But unlike the girl she'd been at nineteen, Lita didn't wait for fate to wave its magical hand. No. She grabbed fate's wrist and shook, *shook*, until the pieces fell into an acceptable pattern. That modus operandi is what had landed her inside a musky, Wilshire division holding cell of LA County's jail system.

Lita didn't have a head for numbers, but was pretty damn sure today would mark the twenty-first time James had bailed her out of a jail-type situation. Looking after the interests of Old News's members was his job. Their relationship, however, fell outside the parameters of a typical musician-manager arrangement. Not that he would ever admit it. No, James simply continued to show up when Lita got into trouble, lecturing her about proper behavior on the way to dropping her off. And leaving. He left *every time*, that distinguished jaw of his firmly set, sunglasses hiding the guilt she knew lurked in his eyes four years later.

Not this time. Last night, Lita had gone above and beyond to ensure this morning wrought one of two outcomes: James quitting, giving up on her like everyone else did eventually, *or* his control finally slipped. One way or another, she wouldn't be in limbo come tonight. She'd been there too long.

Lita stopped jogging when she heard the jingling of the guard's keys. James was right on time, as usual. Her cellmates craned their necks, some coming to their feet in the hopes they were being released. Lita stowed a pang of sympathy and whipped her hair into a quick ponytail. The guard cast a tired-eyed glance in her direction and unlocked the door. "Lita Regina, your bail has been posted."

"Sweet, thanks."

The woman who'd recognized Lita held up a hand for a high-five as she passed through the cell exit. "Aren't you worried about cameras waiting outside?"

Lita slapped the woman's palm. "Not as long as they get my good side." She turned and shook her ass, kicking up snickers around the cell. "Hope everyone gets home for dinner."

Unenthused good-byes followed Lita down the hallway, at the end of which she knew James would be pacing in the waiting area. She already had a sarcastic comment chambered about the wrinkle-free suit he no doubt wore, how out of place he looked. Although, she held out hope he'd been so pissed off by her antics, he'd thrown on jeans for once in his life. James in jeans. Lita ran fingertips down her belly, imagining the way denim would ride his hips. How the smooth circle of the metal button would rest against his stomach all day, warming with his body temperature. *Please, please, let today be the day he stops treating me like a child.* If her body's reaction to thoughts of James were any indication, she was all woman. And she needed the man who'd awakened her needs to tend them.

The guard pushed open the waiting room door, indicating Lita should precede him. When Lita entered the room and saw James, standing with his suited back to her, a smug smile tugged at her lips. God, his tailored glory put their surroundings to shame. Dark hair dusted with salt and pepper at the temples made him more suited to a corporate boardroom than a county jail. The scene reminded Lita of a Marvel Comics movie where the hero tries to blend in among mortals, but is so obviously everyone's savior. Her savior. If he would only allow himself to be. "Well. If it isn't my prom date."

The band manager turned around—and ice formed in Lita's belly, halting her progress halfway across the room. There was one thing she could count on in life—and that was James being furious with her for fucking up. For placing herself in jeopardy. Hell, for getting him out of bed at the crack of dawn. On rare occasions, James tried a new tactic, such as feigned indifference, but he usually broke before they even reached the parking lot. Once he'd attempted sensitivity, but that had failed with flying colors as well. James was a hard, unbendable man. It was one of the reasons she couldn't live without him.

But this? This man waiting for her looked…blank. His arms were at his sides, eyes devoid of feeling as he gave her his typical once-over to determine she'd survived in one piece. A hamster ran on a wheel inside Lita's stomach, faster and faster, when James said nothing. Just *existing* across the room without any of his usual bark or bite.

"James?"

His slate gray eyes lit on the guard, a silent command to leave. Although he held no authority in the jail, the guard turned and lumbered back into the hallway, keys clanking as he went. "Let's go."

She couldn't move. "What's wrong?"

A muscle ticced in his cheek. "We'll need to go out the back exit to avoid the cameras." He left the sentence hanging in the air, turning on a heel to stride from the room. Lita commanded her feet to move, to follow, but catching up to him was like wading through chilled molasses. Maybe this was just a new tactic James had thought up to frighten her. If so, it was working. So much dread had settled in her midsection, it was an effort to walk straight.

At the end of a brightly lit corridor, James stopped at the back entrance and pried open the metal door. He placed one shiny wingtip just outside and checked both directions, presumably for cameras, before gesturing her forward. "All clear."

She started to pass him in the doorway and stopped, craning her neck to meet his stony gaze. "Why won't you talk to me? Why aren't you lecturing me?"

There. It was only a flash, but her proximity affected him, as always. Shoulders tensing, Adam's apple sliding up and down. Yet his tone was dull when he answered. "When has lecturing you ever done any good, Lita?"

"Stop being so cryptic," she whispered. "You're scaring me."

Another tick in his expression, so fleeting she might have imagined it. He stared over her head, though, not directly at her. "Are you hurt in any way?"

"I'm fine."

He gave a single nod and left her in the doorway to unlock the passenger side door. Lita had no choice but to climb inside and engage her seatbelt, as if in a daydream. One from which she desperately needed to wake up. Granted, she hadn't known exactly how James would break—what it would look like—but gut instinct told her this reaction wasn't what she'd been after. She'd wanted James so angry that he'd have no choice but to stop hiding. Stop pretending they weren't denying themselves something vital. Something they both needed.

The hotel she'd been living in since their international tour ended was a fifteen-minute drive from the jail. Silence filled the car, growing denser by the mile until a scream clawed at Lita's throat. "James—"

"You could have been killed."

Finally, a reaction. Disapproval. Lita soaked it in like a sponge, sounding breathless when she said, "I've never seen you this mad." Was this the breaking point? *Please, please let this be it.*

"I don't know what mad is supposed to feel like anymore." His deep voice reached out and smothered her from across the car. "Admit why you did it."

"What do you mean?"

They pulled to a stop at a red light. "You stole a police car last night." His eyes closed, then opened to reveal more nothing. *Nothing.* Just emptiness. "You could have gotten in an accident. Or been shot by the responding officers. And I want to hear you admit why you did it. No more games, Lita."

"I'm not the only one playing games," she whispered.

James was silent for too long. "So you admit it. This is my fault."

"*Yes.*" Hearing herself confess to such recklessness out loud brought home the reality of what she'd done, forcing redness to spread up from her neck. "I don't know how else to get *through* to you." Lita's voice vibrated, her mind scrambling for the right words to make him understand. "This is what it takes just to get a crumb of what I need. The rest of the time you're a statue just watching and watching and *watching* me. At least when you're angry, I can feel a tiny part of what I felt that night."

Gray eyes grew even more shuttered, and his hands flexed on the steering wheel at the forbidden mention of the night they'd met. They pulled into the valet driveway outside her hotel, but James held up a finger to the attendant who stood outside the driver's side window. "I can't give you what you need, Lita." His hand paused on the door handle, his voice grave as she'd ever heard it. "And I will not stay around knowing I'm the reason you continually put yourself at risk."

Lita's reality slowed down, every tick of the imaginary clock sounding like a gong in her ears. Denial expanded, pushing to the furthest edges of her insides, leaving no room for air. "What d-does that mean?"

James stared straight forward as he delivered words that stalled her heart mid-beat. "I've found my replacement. One week from today, I'll no longer be managing Old News."

Chapter Two

James couldn't even look at Lita. Not without feeling as though his stomach were being extracted through his throat. The jail-issued plastic bag containing her possessions was clutched in his right hand as they walked down the carpeted hallway of her hotel. On the way through the revolving glass doors, he'd caught sight of her reflection and knew it would be imprinted on the back of his eyelids for life.

Abandoned. She'd looked abandoned.

James drew a long, deep breath that did nothing to ease or fortify him. It had to be this way. This dysfunctional game between the two of them had gone on too long. He'd found a way to justify it, found a way to stay close by any means necessary, until last night. By simply being in her presence, he put her life at risk. Considering his life's dedication had become the exact opposite four years ago, James had no choice but to get a safe distance away. He hadn't fooled himself into thinking he could give her up completely, but his role in Lita's life now would have to be...peripheral. Much as it would kill him.

Even now, his decision-making remained shoddy, as had been the case since their first meeting. With good-bye on the line, the least wise place James could be was inside Lita's hotel room. Amidst her smell, her clothes...*her*. Always her.

The fucking jig is up. James wasn't a band manager. Nor was he a decent man. The longer he kept the charade up, the harder it would be to walk away from Lita. And since the night he'd taken away any chance of normalcy between them—because once that particular beast was woken, it didn't go back to sleep—he'd known this day would come to pass. His appetite had no business with a fragile girl, twelve years his junior. One who'd raced from one tragedy to another more permanent one. Him.

James didn't question Lita's intelligence. She happened to be the most astute person he'd ever met. A huge heart reserved for her friends and an accurate judge of character. When it came to him, however, she couldn't see below the surface. Had no idea what moved in the shadows of his psyche. Lita wanted something she didn't understand—and worse, James didn't fully understand it either. How could he get a bead on something that constantly shifted and grew, wanting more?

Without thinking, James removed Lita's room key from his pocket and dipped it into the metal reader. As natural as breathing, except it shouldn't be. Lovers kept keys to one another's rooms. He hadn't laid a hand on Lita in four years.

James pushed open the door and set the plastic bag inside, refusing to take one step inside the room. He held out the card for Lita to take as she passed, eyes fastened on the air above her head, but so aware of her nearness his stomach muscles protested from being clenched so tight.

"Oh, god*damn* you." Lita plucked the card from his fingers and hurled it back into the hallway with a muffled scream. "Four years leads to this, huh? You're just going to dump me in this fucking…"—she waved her hands to encompass the hotel—"…rock star purgatory and bail? If you're doing this to teach me a lesson, I will never forgive you, James."

"I'm not." He cleared the cobwebs from his throat. "That's not what this is."

Without looking at Lita, he knew she'd be chewing her bottom lip, leaving teeth marks that would take until nighttime to fade. "I guess we really meant a lot to you if it's this easy. No notice. Just…peace out, suckers."

James swallowed the urge to shake her. "I think you know this is the furthest thing from easy."

"*No.* I don't know *anything*," she shouted before several silent beats passed. "Except that you're a coward. You can't even look me in the eye."

He surged forward, pushing her back against the doorjamb. *Going to break. Too much. I shouldn't have come up here.* He'd made the mistake of looking down into green eyes swimming with moisture, calling her bluff. "Does the thought of you hurting yourself to get my attention make me a coward? Yes? *So be it*, Lita." His fingernails dug into the flesh of his palms. "If something happened to you, I wouldn't make it to the next sunrise."

Lita's body deflated, head falling back. "You can't say something like that and leave," she said, lips hardly moving. "It's cruel."

"I'm a cruel man."

"No." Lita moved into the elegant room, booted feet dragging. A miniature hurricane in a gilded cage. He'd chosen the room himself, another sign of his madness, his need to control her surroundings. Have knowledge of everything she touched. His neck grew hot when she turned, sliding a gaze down his front.

Turning and leaving was imperative at that moment, but he couldn't resist hearing what she would say next. Delaying the good-bye.

"Remember what you called me the first night we met?" She sat down on the edge of the bed. "Before you leave, call me that one more time."

Panic spread dots across his vision. "*No.*"

There was calculation in her expression, but a thread of desperation he'd never witnessed in Lita before. A hint of hysteria. Gone was the sarcasm and wit he'd come to rely on. The difference held him in thrall as she toed off her boots...and peeled the T-shirt over her head, leaving her in a black bra and jeans. *Jesus Christ.* The flesh behind his fly fought to be free of its denim prison. Needing her. Forever needing her. His lungs couldn't find satisfaction, ripping at the air to no avail.

"*Enough.*"

Shaking her head, Lita's tongue danced across her bottom lip. "Maybe I'll ask the new manager to call me that name."

The world turned a dangerous color of red, blood pumping in waves behind his eardrums. James had traversed the room to tower over Lita without a conscious decision. Inside him, something shook, a rattle of chains against a cage, warning him to pull back, but he couldn't. Couldn't. Visions of another man's hands on Lita's skin were all he could process. James's hands circled her biceps, lifting her off the bed and tossing her backward into the mattress's center, finding perverse pleasure in the way her little figure bounced, green eyes widening.

James crawled over Lita, the bed dipping beneath his knees. "The new manager is a woman. Did you think for a second, after everything, that I would overlook a detail so important?" He planted his fists on either side of her head, every inch of his skin feeling raw, exposed. *I'm starving.* "I had no plans to manage a band. Not until you. Now I've spent the last four years deciding where you slept. Where you ate. It's not normal. Not good for you."

"James," she whispered, falling back on the bed beneath him. "We—"

"Stop." He devoured the indentation of her belly button with his gaze, the slope of her ribcage. God, he would sell his soul for a single lick. To feel that shudder against his tongue. "These things I do to keep control, to keep you in places that allow me to sleep at night…that need only grows. Eventually I would stop you from being Lita and you would hate me for it. I would hate me, too."

"I couldn't." She turned her head and laid her lips on his forearm, severing his heart in eighteen places. "I push you to it. I'll stop. I promise I'll stop pushing if you stay. If you just…kiss me, you'll know that everything is going to be fine. *Please?*"

Begging was so uncharacteristic for Lita, so unusual, that James wasn't prepared for the pleasure that skated over his senses like a revelation. He loved hearing her pleas? God, what a sickness he had. "I want *bad* things." Was that *his* voice? "*Need* them."

Lita pushed up on her elbows, bringing their mouths close. "Bring it."

Her husky challenge untethered urges he'd held in check too long. Electric energy scratched at the insides of his veins, an unnamed force gripping him by the nape. If he didn't release some of the mounting pressure, he would implode. What was left of his common sense twisted around, turned inside out, reasoning that if he exposed some of the need to Lita, she would make this easer. She would stop begging him to finally fuck her and start begging him to leave.

Too late to turn back. Coming to his knees above her, James curled his right hand around her throat, exerting just enough pressure to keep her still. Pink, teeth-marked lips popped open to suck in a breath. A breath James could feel being inhaled against his palm. *So perfect.* "There's my little plaything." He adjusted his grip. "Is that what you wanted to hear?"

Lita's eyelids fluttered down to conceal her gaze, an acknowledgment of the pet name he'd growled in her ear so long ago in the dark. Just once. But it had been enough to remain poised on his tongue ever since, pleading to be uttered aloud.

James leaned down to inspect the curve of her cheek. "If another man called you his plaything, Lita, I would *gut* him."

Beneath him, Lita's stomach dipped and lifted, making contact with his abdomen and calling attention to the position of his ready cock. A few quick maneuvers of their clothing and he'd be seated in her look-but-do-not-touch pussy. And *Christ*, he'd looked. She'd paraded that sweet spot around him in every manner of thin material known to man. Spandex, ripped denim, threadbare cotton. Just for his eyes. His torment.

"You haven't been fucked since we met. I've seen to it. Do you know how?" Damning himself, James dropped his hips into the cradle of her thighs, choking back the moan that emerged from his mouth, savoring the answering moan Lita let loose. "I put the fear of God into them. I paid them to fuck off. I've used my fists on a few that proved…overeager. Whatever it took."

Craving the sight of her body, James released her throat and trailed fingertips down the center of her chest, tracing the front snap of her bra. His mouth turned to a desert at the idea of sucking her nipples, but no…*no*, that would be too sweet. Too pleasurable. She would like it. And his mission was to make her understand. This…him…was not what she wanted. With regret screaming in his head, James trailed his fingers lower, down her trembling belly, to tuck inside the waistband of Lita's jeans. *Not here, either. No touching here.*

"Who's going to stop them now?" Her winded—and somewhat hesitant—

question interrupted his fevered thoughts. "The men. Who will stop them?"

Fuuuuck. The denim ripped inside his shaking fist, his rebelling mind demanding more of the satisfying sound. He yanked down the zipper behind her already tattered fly, giving himself a leveraging handhold before tearing the jeans down her body. It left the very tops of her thighs exposed, along with the little white triangle of her panties. "Stop *provoking* me."

"No," Lita breathed. "I *won't.*"

Feeling the remaining threads of his control begin to fray, James slipped a hand over her mouth to silence her. *Show her. Show her you're an animal.* "Don't make a sound," James rasped into her hair, rubbing his open mouth over the soft strands. He shoved her thighs apart with his knees and bore down hard, pumping dry against her barely covered pussy. "If you scream or try to fight me, you'll only make it worse for yourself."

Lita's body went still as death beneath him. This was it. Finally over. Four years of trying to be someone she could count on, someone she could feel safe with against all odds, and he'd ruined everything. Even though that had been his goal, the reality was like razor blades—

She began to struggle, hips jerking in an obvious attempt to buck him off. James's head flew up, horror puncturing his sternum. Oh God, but there was more. *More.* An urge to pin down her writhing form that swarmed his head, buzzing like a colony of bees. His girl wanted to be free of him? Wanted other men to call her pet names? Didn't she know his sanity would bleed out through his ears?

Get off her. You have to get off.

Lita's knee came up and dug into his ribs, making him grunt. Why were her eyes closed? If she would just *look* at him—what? Would he reassure her as always? No, it would be false. This was the man she'd been sharing oxygen with, and it was time she knew.

He'd been picturing this scene since day one. *Seal the deal.*

James released her covered mouth, wincing when her breath emerged labored, her hands flying to his shoulders, fingers digging in *hard*. "James, *please.*"

"Did you think I was being noble? Simply giving your body a chance to mature?" He pinned her flailing wrists on either side of her hips, trailing rough kisses between her breasts, down her stomach to end at her mound. His hungry lips hovered there a moment to pay homage, to warm the sacred flesh with a release of breath. "Jesus, Lita. When we met, you barely looked old enough to have your driver's license. And still—*still*—I did those bad things to you in the dark. Didn't I?"

Above him, Lita whimpered. Again, she attempted to free herself, but he held fast. "Wait, I...I—"

"You should have known back then I was an *indecent* man." He licked her pussy through the white cotton panties, groaning when his cock throbbed. Inflicting pain on himself, he licked Lita's covered perfection again and again, like she was a fucking ice cream cone. Dragging himself away from her taste made him crazed. *Mine. It tastes like mine.* "All this time, you've treated me like a protector." He pushed her thighs open. "But I was the one you should have been afraid of."

"N-no, I'm not."

Liar. Her quavering voice was a dead giveaway. That was her stubbornness talking, her inability to lose a battle. *Finish it.* James widened his jaw and dropped his teeth down over her pussy, covering as much as his mouth would allow. Which due to her petite body was—fucking hell—*all* of it. He didn't bite right away, wanting to feel her reaction. Wanting to feel her realization of *James is going to bite me between my legs.* Her limbs were shaking in his hands, tiny gasps sparking in the air around them. In degrees, he closed his teeth, tighter and tighter until she screamed.

"James!"

At the desire brought flooding forth by Lita's panicked cry, shame rocked him. Hard. *What am I doing? What am I doing to this incredible girl?* She'd trusted him. She'd let him be a part of her life. He'd caged her brilliance and since walking into this room, he'd dragged her into his twisted mind, kicking and—*screaming*.

James was off the bed and across the room in seconds. "I'm sorry. *Goddammit*." Hands braced on his hips, he faced the door. Couldn't look or her disgust, fear, disappointment, would haunt him the rest of his life. "I never want to hurt you, Lita. No one should *ever* hurt you."

"Don't you dare leave now," she sobbed behind him. "Don't you *dare*."

He almost laughed, but it would have ruptured the organs left functioning inside him. The girl was too fearless for her own good. Did she think she could talk him through this and fix him? Yes, she likely did. Likely thought he just needed a mental ass kicking to pull his shit together. And then…God, she would forgive him for what he'd just done—holding her down and acting out his darkest fantasy. No way he'd ever be able to live with her apology, the added self-hatred that would follow. "I know it's hard to believe a word I say after what I just did. But until this morning, everything I've ever done was in your best interest. Please believe that. You're going to be better—safer—without me."

"*No*. Don't—"

"Good-bye, Lita.

Feeling as though he'd been submerged in water, James staggered from the hotel room, sweat breaking out along his forehead and upper lip. It hurt leaving her, hurt to increase the distance. Every. Step. *Hurt*. Felt wrong. Knowing Lita would follow him, James skipped the elevator and took the stairwell. His phone began buzzing before he'd even left the hotel. Knowing it was Lita and he couldn't answer, James nonetheless pulled out his phone just to see her name on the screen. But it wasn't Lita at all, the actual identity of the caller slowing his step. After a slight hesitation, he answered.

"Mother."

Chapter Three

Four years earlier

Lita stared at the stranger across the fancy, gleaming hotel table.

The stranger stared back.

Good lord, the man was...incredible. Big, commanding, sharp. Distinguished, too, with the beginnings of silver threading the hair above his ears. If she were given to embarrassment, he would have been gorgeous enough to inspire a twinge of self-consciousness, since at present, she was shoveling donuts into her gob like a shipwreck survivor who'd just been rescued from a deserted island. In a way, she had been rescued downstairs in the bar. So why did she feel like she'd been sent back out to sea...in an even more turbulent storm?

When she'd ventured into the bar tonight, she'd envisioned herself being grudgingly assisted and taken upstairs by some checked-out, soulless asshole, of which there were plenty in Los Angeles. This man was the furthest thing from checked out. He was so present. A buzz crawled up her skin the longer he stared. He'd barely strung a sentence together since he'd carried her into the room, splashing cold water from the bathroom sink onto her face. They'd conversed enough for him to ascertain what she'd like to eat—chocolate donuts, chocolate anything—which he'd promptly ordered from room service.

But that voice. That clipped, dictator voice had made her shake.

Especially when he'd called to her through the slightly ajar bathroom door as she'd showered, making sure consciousness hadn't failed her again.

Lita swallowed half of a donut without chewing, brushing the crumbs off her fluffy, white hotel robe, before picking up another one. "Aren't you going to *eat one?"*

"No."

Another shiver wracked her spine. "What's your name?"

"James." His eyes snapped with emotions she could barely pin down before they shifted or expanded or disappeared. "And yours?"

"Lita." She sipped her hot chocolate. "Thank you for this."

"You're welcome." He laid a flat hand on the table. They both looked down at it, as if it were a third party interrupting them. "You came along at an unfortunate time, Lita." His head gave a tight jerk, jaw clenching. "I haven't been feeling like myself."

"Really." She set the donut down, her stomach executing a series of flips. Nervous ones, but not the type that made her want to run. Not the type she'd experienced before. These were hotter, fuller, curious. "How do you feel...instead?"

"I have hunger." His dark gaze swung up, gluing her to the plush leather seat. "I don't know if it can be fed like yours."

What was going on here? Lita felt almost hypnotized, lured in by his rasping, cultured voice. She recognized interest and arousal in men, had it directed at her often, but this? This was utter famishment. He reminded her of a vampire who'd been in hiding from the sun, unable to hunt. And now a deer lay before him, vital and tempting, life flowing through its veins. She was the deer.

Man. How crazy were her thoughts right now? The lack of food must have gone to her head. After the trouble she'd just escaped, she shouldn't care what went on under another man's surface. Shouldn't allow this odd, instantaneous attachment to take hold.

The fuller her stomach became, though, the more her thoughts cleared. The more of James she saw. His interest in her, as he watched her mouth chew, was almost as thick as the leash around his neck, keeping him in place. If the lights in the room weren't so dim, she could probably make it out. Strain bracketed his masculine mouth and he appeared to be swallowing golf balls down the column of his powerful throat. One...after...another.

"How did you get so hungry?" James asked, his tone suggesting he was reclining back onto a bed of nails.

Lita rejected the outside ugliness from entering the room. "I could ask you the same thing." Her legs were steady as she stood and rounded the table, compelled by some force she couldn't deny. Maybe it was his clear attempt to restrain himself, to fight the attraction so obvious between them. She stopped beside James, but he stayed still as stone. "I'm full. What happens now?"

His eyelids drooped, fist mashing against his forehead. "Go."

That single, tortured word caught her in the chest. God, he was holding back so much. What would happen when it roared out?

Why was she trembling with the need to find out?

There was danger lurking beneath this man's surface. Also known as the last thing a homeless girl wanting to turn her luck around needed.

Too bad danger was the only thing that had ever made her feel alive.

Lita walked past James to the lamp and flipped off the gentle light before returning to his tense figure, sliding between his outstretched legs...and opening the robe. "Feed yourself."

The air crackled as James stood slowly, so slowly, rising to his full height. When Lita glimpsed his changed expression, she realized that—at her invitation—a change had snapped through him like a cracking whip, despite the way he rose without hurry. The vampire's dirt nap had officially ended and the invisible leash was no more. Power rippled over his beautiful body as it pressed close, a hand finding her hip inside the robe, squeezing, his mouth sliding against her ear.

His breath went choppy after issuing a single unexpected command.

"Crawl."

* * * *

Lita had a blister on her ankle. It rubbed and rubbed against the back of her red Converse, growing angrier and bloodier by the hour. All it would take to fix the injury was a Band-Aid, but she didn't have time for that shit. Didn't have time to take her shoe off, remove the protective strip from its paper packaging and apply it. Performing such a practical task wouldn't make sense when the world around her had been painted different colors, and normal, everyday activities proved impossible. Sleep wasn't happening and the act of procuring food seemed like a monumental effort just to feel sick afterward, so she simply walked. Walked and walked around Los Angeles with headphones covering her ears, the star of her own depressing music montage.

Empty didn't begin to explain the sensation beneath her bones. She felt...dead. In a way, she *was*. This life, the band, had all been orchestrated by James. Their conversation the morning after they met was still vivid in her memory. Crystal clear and sparkling like drinking glasses fresh from a dishwasher. James had asked her, "What do you *do*, Lita?" And she'd answered, "I drum."

That was all it took. He'd found a lead singer and a bass player within two weeks, throwing them together inside rented studio space, and thus, Old News was born. James's life prior to that time was still a mystery to her. To everyone. If what he'd said before leaving was true, his every action over the last four years had been in the interest of helping her. Out of guilt? Kindness? Lita didn't know. But none of it seemed real without him standing at her back, watching her from behind dark sunglasses.

Holy, holy shit, she *missed* him. Okay, they'd had their fair share of squabbles and arguments. *More* than their fair share. But there'd been some incredible moments wedged in there. Like the time the tour bus had blown a fan belt in Mexico and they'd shared a six-pack on the roof, staring at the sky and waiting for help to arrive. Or the time she'd convinced him to walk out on stage and sing the encore with Old News, which he'd started with a scowl on his face, but ended up smiling.

Dammit. The way he'd left was unfair and *stupid*, and she wanted to rage at him. Fine, he'd been right about one thing. Lita hadn't understood the intensity of his needs. He'd blindsided her with the force and sharp quality of them. They were complicated and dark. But her response had been...light. The blinding, white light of an atomic blast. She'd *liked* James holding her down and saying those frightening words into her hair. Liked the abrasive tone of his voice, liked her strength running out, little by little, until she could only submit. That almost unbearable lift in her stomach, the glorious clearing of her mind...she'd been chasing that feeling by causing trouble for so long, never quite achieving it.

He'd left before she could get a handle on her runaway desires, what they meant, how to voice them. If he'd just given her a minute, she would have begged for more. Would have reassured him that the trust between them was still intact and nothing could damage it. Nothing except him leaving. Leaving her to this existence he'd created and managed from behind the scenes, but neglected to leave the instructions behind.

James wasn't even home, so they couldn't properly have it out. His old Mustang wasn't in the driveway of his house in Santa Monica. Hadn't been for three days. He'd vanished. And part of her worried that starving nineteen-year-old girl had fabricated his existence in the first place. After all, who gave up their own life in exchange for some scrawny, homeless girl's success? No person she'd met before him, that was for damn sure. Her own parents hadn't been in the picture since she turned sixteen, having moved down to Mexico with the settlement they'd received when Lita's mother broke her ankle on a public bus. After that, she'd floated, living with friends until meeting her one and only boyfriend.

Shaking off the uncomfortable memory of how *that* unhealthy relationship came to a close, Lita turned her focus to step one in tracking down James. And she *would* track his sexy backside down, even if it were just to give him hell. But she hoped it would end in more. It had to.

Sarge Purcell was the lead singer of Old News and the closest thing resembling a friend to James. Which is why Lita was stomping up the driveway of his newly purchased beach house at eight o'clock in the morning. If anyone knew where their manager had gone, it would be Sarge. She felt a tad guilty for interrupting his first official week in Los Angeles since returning from New Jersey with his girlfriend, Jasmine, but hey. Desperate times.

Lita rapped on the fogged glass front door and waited. The sound of crashing waves from behind the house should have been soothing, but they only sounded like bombs going off in her ears, exacerbating the headache pumping behind her eyes for days without pause. *Just focus on this one thing.*

The lead singer opened the door in a pair of gray boxer briefs, but Lita didn't even blink. When you've lived on a tour bus with someone, modesty goes extinct with a quickness. Sarge's hair was finger-raked and haphazard as usual, but Lita had a feeling it was Jasmine's fingers that had been doing the raking. Lita's theory was confirmed when Jasmine stumbled through the living room behind Sarge, wearing nothing but a white sheet.

"Hey, Jasmine," Lita called, but her voice came out sounding thready, since she hadn't spoken since…when? Since James left? "Sorry to have interrupted the sexing."

Sarge grinned, displaying the reason his face ended up on countless magazine covers. "Ah, it's fine. You'd be interrupting that no matter when you showed up."

"Don't take this the wrong way, Sargeant, but you've turned into a smug bastard."

He threw a proud look over his shoulder, sending a smiling Jasmine snuggling into the couch cushions. "If a man wasn't smug over landing that woman, he'd be an idiot."

An ache formed so quickly in Lita's chest, she sucked in a breath. "Yeah, well. I'm trying to make my own bastard look smug. You want to help me out with that?"

Sarge's expression lost its humor. "I don't know where James is, if that's why you're here." He crossed his arms and leaned on the doorframe. "What happened between you two?"

Lita's laugh sounded full of liquid. "I wouldn't even tell you after a bottle of tequila." She pushed past her bandmate into the house, heading straight for the kitchen. "Speaking of tequila, where is yours?"

"Cabinet above the toaster," Jasmine said, her voice muffled.

"Thanks."

Lita busied herself pouring the golden liquor into a coffee cup while Sarge went and put on a T-shirt. When he joined her in the kitchen, she'd already knocked back two shots. Sarge took a seat on a barstool, while watching her with obvious concern. "So it's true. He's stepping down as manager. I honestly thought he was screwing with me."

"So you *have* talked to him."

Sarge shook his head. "Voicemail. He doesn't answer when I call back."

Tears pressed behind Lita's eyelids, pissing her off. Goddammit. She'd never cried this many days in a row, including the week she'd binged on *Grey's Anatomy* while driving through Europe on the tour bus. "Do you know where his family lives?"

"I don't even know if he has any family."

Lita tossed back another two fingers of tequila. "How do we

know exactly nothing about him after *four years*?"

Sarge scrubbed a hand over his face. "Maybe that's how he wants it, Lita."

"That's not how *I* want it." When her voice broke, she closed her eyes. "Please, you have to help me find his big, dumb face. I can fix this."

Her bandmate reached out, setting his big hand atop her head. "You know we'll do everything we can."

"Thanks," Lita mumbled, shrugging free of her friend's comforting gesture. She didn't want to be comforted or soothed. It would only be temporary until she found James and filled in the massive crater he'd left gaping in her middle.

Jasmine came into the kitchen, walking right into the crook of Sarge's outstretched arm, as if they'd been apart way too long. "Don't you have security guards who travel with Old News to shows?" The gorgeous ex-factory worker split a look between them. "A lot of those guys are ex-cops. Maybe they can help?"

For the first time in days, Lita felt the blessed spark of hope. "That might actually work. If someone else does that favor asking." She plunked the empty coffee mug into the sink. "They all hate me because I'm always ordering the crowd to mosh for their lives. Doesn't exactly make their job easy."

"No, I wouldn't think so," Jasmine said, obviously fighting laughter. "I can help make the calls. James helped get me to Sarge when I almost lost him. I'd love to return the favor."

After that, there was no one in the room but Sarge and Jasmine. The lead singer looked like he might organize a sacrifice of himself on an altar to the gods just to thank them for creating his girlfriend. Jasmine couldn't stop staring at his mouth. And yeah…they were seconds from boning on the kitchen island, so Lita shoved the bottle of tequila into her purse and skirted past them toward the front door. "I'll be down on the beach getting shit faced when you guys are done."

Once outside, she took a fortifying breath and slipped the cell phone from her back pocket. She couldn't sit still and wait for other people to help her anymore. Something had to be done *now* before she went crazy. Maybe just then, buzzed on tequila and emotionally drained wasn't a good time to start owning up to her mistakes and acting like an adult, but time kept passing, passing, passing without James, and that felt like a horrible travesty. A waste of valuable minutes.

It was time to take control of her own life. Her own fate. No one was responsible for Lita's happiness but her.

She went down to the beach and started making calls.

* * * *

James sat outside the hospital, hands clasped between his splayed legs. He'd left his cell phone back at his roadside motel in an effort to allay temptation. For so long, he'd had the device holstered like a six-shooter, ready to draw if someone needed him. No, not just *someone*. Lita. He felt naked without news of her right at his fingertips. Several times since driving back to his hometown of Modesto, he'd checked the gossip websites and police blotters, praying nothing about Lita would show. His habits were firmly ingrained and he couldn't trust himself yet to stay away should she land in hot water.

So far, there had been nothing, apart from news agencies following up on her recent arrest and subsequent release from jail. She hadn't called or e-mailed, telling him he'd finally succeeded in scaring her off.

Good. He'd always known she was smart.

James breathed through the horror of having scared the one person he'd dedicated his life to saving from pain. Relief would come eventually, along with the conviction he'd done what was right. If it didn't, at least he'd know Lita was happy. Somewhere without him.

A shadow filled the sunlit walkway in front of the bench where he sat, temporarily lifting him from mental torture. He lifted his head to find his mother running a Kleenex beneath her eyes. "How is he?"

"Better," she responded with a sigh. "Still no movement on the right side of his body, but he's communicating with the white board and marker. He won't try speaking just yet...I think because it feels so unnatural with only half his mouth."

James gave a tight nod. "Still no desire to see me, I assume?"

His mother's sympathetic look was unbearable, so James stood and paced away. He'd been home for six days, following the phone call from his mother informing James that his father had a stroke. Over a decade had passed since the last time he'd been face to face with the man—frankly, he'd been content to remain in contact with his mother only, when there was an occasion or major holiday. Unfortunately, the family landscaping business didn't run without his father, so his mother had begged James—their only child—to step in until the company's manager returned from a family reunion trip overseas. Regardless of James's non-relationship with his father, there'd been some solace in being needed after relinquishing his title as manager to Old News. As protector to Lita.

Working with his hands had given James some place to direct the restless energy, so he'd taken a labor role in addition to the managerial responsibilities. The last six mornings, he'd spent digging trenches, planting trees, hauling rubble. And six afternoons in a row, he'd been refused entry to his father's hospital room.

The sidewalk outside the hospital had begun to fill up, presumably with a shift change, if the amount of personnel was any indication. People rushed up the walkway to take advantage of the final hour of visiting time before the dinner break. An unnamable tug of consciousness pointed out an anomaly among the moving mass of people. A flash of life, of static, that didn't belong with the rest. Sort of like déjà vu that wouldn't stop, just looping back and around, keeping him edgy.

Holding up a finger for his mother to pause in the vocal listing of medication the doctor had administered to her husband, James turned in a circle, the pulses in his wrists hammering. When his gaze lit on the cause of his body's visceral reaction, it took James a moment to believe what his eyes were telling him.

Lita marched up the hospital walkway, all out *war* written on her beautiful face. The way she sometimes looked during a drum solo. Concentrated brilliance. Jesus God, how? How had he made it this long without a glimpse of her? James took an involuntary step in Lita's direction, his body obeying instinct. And instinct said, *I need to go get mine.* There was nothing but bone-melting fulfillment upon his first eyeful of the girl who ruled him. Always would—no denying that fact. But when his brain registered the entire picture, his mission stalled out, giving way to an avalanche of *other.* Lust, denial, anger. They whipped around him like a whirlpool, sucking him down into an ocean of chaos.

An all-too-familiar thrift shop outfit covered Lita's body, cheap material hugging her swaying hips, the crop top's leather fringe ending at her belly button. The outfit she'd worn the night they met.

When Lita's Converse scuffed to a stop on the sidewalk in front of him, James's fists were shaking with the need to get hands around some part of her and *keep.* A roar escaped him instead. *"What are you doing here?"* He barely registered his mother's startled gasp beside him. "What kind of game are you playing?"

"Game?" Green eyes blazing, she turned around to execute a stiff karate-type kick in the air before facing him again with her shirt's fringe still swinging. "How dare you call this a game when I've spent *six days* and four bus transfers tracking you down."

An invisible hand squeezed his neck. "Why?"

"Why." Shaking her head, she looked downright disgusted with him. "I'm so mad at you, James, my mad grew a second head and ate the first one."

James realized two things at once. One, he'd always classified his feelings for Lita as sheer obsession, but the fact was, he was achingly, irrevocably in love with her. Which meant letting her go would be infinitely harder than his fool self had thought. And two, blood soaked clear through the back of her favorite Converse, so much that it left droplets in her wake on the concrete sidewalk. "Why…" He had to take a moment to formulate the question, the sight of injury on her person was so abhorrent to his peace of mind. *Can't breathe.* "Why the fuck are you bleeding?"

"Is this your mother or something? It *is*, isn't it? We're arguing in front of your mother." Lita threw up her hands and sagged at the same time. "So be it, James. Your family will think I'm crazy and that's too bad. I *am* crazy. If you want to get rid of me, you better start working on a restraining order." A passing group of nurses were staring at Lita, bottled drinks in their hands. "Hey. Yeah. I know. The crazy has arrived. Why don't you just...drink your stupid lemonade, huh?"

Only half of her words had penetrated the graying haze surrounding James, his sole focus on her right ankle. "I can't have this conversation when you're bleeding."

"I'm *always* bleeding when you're standing in front of me," she said, chin lifting. "You just can't see it."

His hurt lurched. "Lita..."

She stomped the injured foot, nearly spiraling him into a heart attack. "Yeah, I know. I say things like that now. Get used to it."

The whole situation was getting out of hand. James didn't know what her goals were in traveling three hundred miles, but she'd wasted her time. He'd finally found the strength to direct his brand of destruction away from Lita and seeing her, hearing her, smelling her, nearly touching her, was fucking with his resolve in a catastrophic way. "Why are you wearing that?" James gritted out.

She glanced down at her attire, as if riding four buses with both thighs completely exposed was a mere afterthought. When she looked up at him again, those teeth were busy chewing away at her bottom lip, stirring his neglected male flesh. It didn't help matters when Lita stepped closer, dropping her voice to a whisper. "I don't think I should answer that in front of your mother, James." She let out a shaky exhale. "Anyway, you...you're wearing *jeans*."

God, how could she make a statement of fact sound like those final strained words before an orgasm? His cock wasn't handling the public sidewalk seduction well at all, thickening inside the restrictive denim, his balls weighed down in a hot rush. On top of his aroused state, Lita's injury demanded his attention. Now.

"Mother, I will call you later."

James stepped forward and scooped Lita up against his chest. Something he'd done on more than one occasion when shows got too rowdy, but it felt very different now. Instead of her protector, he was a predator carrying her away from the light. Away from normalcy, where she belonged.

"How is your father?"

He felt her breath against his neck clear down to his toes.

"Awake. Alive."

"Okay." She laid her lips against his pulse. "Do you want to talk about why you weren't inside when I pulled up?"

"No." He jerked away when every instinct screamed to lean in, absorb the touch. Tell her everything. "How did you find me?"

Lita laid her head on his shoulder, running him through with an invisible sword. "I had a little help from our security team."

"Impossible. You make their life hell."

"Yes, I know. They might have mentioned it a few hundred times." She exhaled, ruffling the hair at the back of his neck. The best feeling he'd had in six goddamn days. "Old News is playing two bat mitzvahs and one wedding this summer. For free. I haven't met our new manager yet, but I doubt that will earn me a spot as teacher's pet."

Despite the situation with his father and knowing this moment with Lita couldn't last, James almost laughed. "Only you."

When they reached his Mustang, he noticed her ankle was dripping onto the sidewalk and didn't manage to swallow the gruff sound that left him. "How could you let it get so bad?"

It took her a moment to release his shoulders when he set her down on the passenger seat. "I think...I thought if I hurt enough, you would feel it and come back. I wanted to punish you, too. For leaving." She crossed her arms over her middle. "The only way I could do that was to punish myself."

His hand curled into a fist on the car's roof. "Can't you see how wrong that is?"

"Yes. We were both a little wrong." She held his gaze from below. "But I'm going to make it right."

Chapter Four

Lita knew her plan was a gamble. And she used the word *plan* loosely.

For all she knew, it could make things worse between her and James. If such a thing were possible. The ride to the motel had been silent, his huge hands flexing on the steering wheel as they always did when Lita rode shotgun. Upon arrival, he'd ordered her to stay put in the passenger seat and for once, she'd put up no argument. The tension in him was a living thing as he rounded the Mustang's bumper to jerk her door open. Then she was back in his capable arms, being carried across the twilight-draped parking lot.

"So. I think things went well with your mom."

James said nothing, gaze glued to the motel as they approached.

"On the way here, the bus stopped at a Dairy Queen and someone thought I was Carly Rae Jepsen. Again."

The man wasn't amused. "You still haven't explained what you're wearing."

"Be patient. I'm getting there." Lita took a deep breath, hoping to stall until they were inside the room and he couldn't bar her entry. She played with the collar of his T-shirt, her belly flipping at the dark chest hair peeking out. In four years, she'd never seen him shirtless and hoped that wouldn't be the case much longer. When James set her down gently in front of a rusted, teal door and dug for the room key in his pocket, she watched the denim stretch across the bulge at his lap, the waistband dipping low. "I want to say something profound here, but I can only think of terrible pickup lines."

"Please don't say them."

"Were those jeans on sale?" She pointed at the closed door. "Because I know where we can get them one hundred percent off."

"Jesus." He turned the key in the lock and shoved open the door. "I'm glad *you're* getting a kick out of this."

She gasped when he picked her up again, but recovered quickly and glanced around the basic, no frills room. "Maybe I'm just nervous."

His stride broke just inside the door, the dark stillness enfolding them. "You're... nervous with me."

Lita threw her arms around his neck and held. "That's not what I meant. Or maybe it is. But not in the way you're thinking."

He continued his stalk toward the bathroom, throwing on the fluorescent light and setting Lita down on the sink. "Explain."

Now or never. Lita opened her mouth to relay her thoughts, but James chose that moment to remove her right shoe, sending pain slicing up her calf. "*Ohh, God.*"

James dropped into a crouch to inspect the damage, alarm written across his chiseled features. It was bad. She knew the way his skin paled, the way his voice emerged strangled. "If you were trying to punish me, Lita, it fucking worked."

Shit. She was losing him. To anyone else, he would have appeared closed off since her arrival in town, but she knew him better than that. He'd been on the brink of finally talking to her. So she had to work fast before he retreated, risk be damned. "I wore this outfit because...I know you feel guilty about what happened that first night. So we're going to go back and do it right." She curled her fingers into the cotton T-shirt covering his broad shoulders, tugging, until he finally stood, watching her with a hooded expression. "Show me how you would do it differently, James."

His gray eyes darkened, the sink groaning beneath his grip. "It won't fix what's wrong with me."

"No." She wet her parched lips. "It might fix what's broken

with us, though."

Oh, he wanted to take the opportunity and run. There was no denying it. Not when he grew winded looking down at her thighs, her bare midriff. He'd been in check around Lita so long, resisting even her most brazen advances. Maybe it was their dynamic as musician-manager having changed, or maybe it was the feeling of isolation provided by the silent motel. But she saw his hunger, not just for her, but to replace the memory of their night together with one he could stand. One he could live with. "Have..." His throat worked. "Have you eaten?"

Lita shook her head.

James's face remained impassive as he set to work cleaning her ankle, wiping it clean and holding a towel against the cut until it stopped bleeding. All the while, his gaze coasted up her legs, dipping to the space between where she knew the cream-colored material of her thong could be seen. She leaned back against the bathroom mirror and arched her back, letting him peruse her breasts through the awful polyester, focusing on keeping her breathing even.

When he finally spoke, his voice was so raw Lita was transported back to that night in the Los Angeles hotel. He sounded edgy. Just a hint pissed off. "Can you stand in the shower?"

"Yes."

James nodded once. "Get clean while I find something to feed you." He turned to leave the bathroom, but paused with one hand on the doorjamb. "If we do this, you need words. And you'll need to remember them, Lita. I want you to say Beverly Wilshire if I need to stop. Do you understand?"

Breathe. Breathe. "Yes, I understand."

He nodded once, his voice dropping another devastating octave. "Put the outfit back on when you're finished."

Without waiting for Lita's response, James left the room, closing the door with a decisive click. She slipped off the sink, careful not to agitate her ankle, and started the shower. As steam filled the white tile room, she looked at herself in the mirror, noticing the red staining her cheeks. The excitement dancing in her eyes. How long would it take him to touch her? Anticipation blazed through her veins, vitalizing, electrifying. A significant part of her wanted to goad James to lose control, because while he'd roared over her like a freight train during their one physical encounter, he roused something hot and dangerous. Something she'd spent four years trying to recapture, to no avail. But no. If she forced him to repeat actions he regretted, she would regret it tomorrow. Staying the course was tonight's game plan.

She'd been in the shower for a handful of minutes when James returned, slamming the door and making her jump. She soaped herself faster, wanting to hurry and join him in the room before he changed his mind.

James walked into the bathroom.

He came to a stop inches from the glass stall, watching as the soap rinsed from her body, down to the drain. For a heavy, breathless moment, he stared at her breasts, belly, and backside. Not moving. Just when she thought he'd frozen into marble, he heaved a shaking exhale that fogged the glass and twisted lust in Lita's belly. She swore his warm breath reached her through the barrier, the way it turned her nipples to points, forcing a moan past her damp lips.

Unsure how to proceed with this wickedly intense James of her memory, Lita turned off the shower and stepped from the stall to dry herself with a scratchy white towel, rubbing the ends of her hair to remove excess water. His cool began to slip when she stepped into her discarded skirt, dragging it up her damp legs, situating the garment even higher than usual. The material clung to her hips and buttocks like seeking hands, turning her on, readying her body.

Deciding to forgo the bra, Lita tugged the matching shirt down over her head. "Are you going to say anything?"

"Go eat," James growled. "Before I eat you first."

Game plan. Game plan. Lita launched herself into the bedroom, noticing the box of donuts immediately. Of its own accord, her hand lifted to clutch at her chest, an attempt to soothe the sudden hammering beneath. "Chocolate?"

His footsteps drew up behind her. "I always wondered why you picked donuts that night. I told you I'd bring you anywhere."

She swallowed. "You were so intimidating in your suit. I thought maybe if I saw frosting on your fingers…"

"I wouldn't be so scary?" His hand settled on her hip, giving it a squeeze, as if testing her resilience. "It didn't take me long to disappoint you, did it?"

Knowing from experience that her reassurances to the contrary would do no good, Lita went to the basic, wooden table and selected a chocolate donut from the box. When she took her first bite, she faced James, remembering that night how he'd watched her chew across the plastic Dunkin Donuts booth, encouraging her to eat more. That night, she'd polished off four donuts and two paper cups of room service hot chocolate before saying uncle. Now, she could barely manage to keep half the pastry down, thanks to the butterfly rave taking place in her stomach.

"You're done?"

"Yes." Before he could argue, she rushed to speak. "What would you have done next? If you could go back."

He looked away on a harsh laugh before gray eyes blazed back to hers. "I wouldn't have behaved like a sick motherfucker. Wouldn't have made you crawl across the floor to me and beg. I wouldn't have—" His words broke off when Lita came toward him. "What are you doing?"

She didn't think, *couldn't* think around the regret and pain radiating from his powerful frame. Nor could she restrain herself after hearing him *finally* acknowledge the fantasy she'd reenacted so many times in her mind. Over and over. So she went up on her bare toes and kissed his hard mouth….and…*ohhh*. Just like that, they were having their first kiss. *Good Lord.* The first taste of James was so outrageously right and delicious and sexual, she sagged against him, fingers twisting in his shirt to keep balanced. Man. He was coarse, unfiltered man. He tore his mouth away on a groan of her name before diving back in, yanking her off the floor and flush against his body.

Desperation gripped Lita when she felt his erection, a mountain of denim prodding her belly. She scrambled up his muscular body, wrapping thighs around already rolling hips, and received that first upward thrust between her legs. A pop of color decorated her vision, a montage of blinking lights. Their mouths ravaged harder, James the clear aggressor now, with Lita struggling to accommodate his hunger. Loving it. Figuring out new ways to greet his tongue, stroke it. She couldn't get her mouth open wide enough. More. All. *All, all, all.*

When James broke away, she twined her fingers in his hair to pull him back, but he evaded, drilling her with tortured eyes. "I spanked you so damn hard. You were lost...hungry. You needed help and I fucking failed you."

"*No.* How can you say that after everything you've done?"

His hands roamed down her back, stopping just before her backside, clutching the hem of her shirt. "Nothing can fix it. Oh, God. You had...bruises." He closed his eyes. "You ran away from someone who hurt you and I did the same thing. I was just another monster."

Lita kissed his mouth until he looked at her again. "I made you leave the lights off so you wouldn't see them. *I* did that." Another soft kiss. "You didn't know until the next morning. And it's not the same."

"Yes," he grated against her mouth. "It is."

"No. I enjoyed it. I...loved when you did it. The way you did it. We both wanted everything that happened. I'm sorry you don't remember it that way."

She didn't realize they'd moved until her back landed on the mattress. James's weight came down on top of her and she almost screamed at the necessity of that gravitational pressing of their bodies. Like a drink of cold water in the desert. In the sexiest move of all time, he pinned Lita with his hips and whipped the T-shirt over his head, baring his rough-hewn body. God, it was so hot, heat went straight to her clit, sensitizing the flesh, making her whimper.

"You don't think I know you enjoyed it?" He drew her top up, past her breasts, baring them to his stark hunger. "You've spent every minute since that night trying to tempt me back here. Pressing your tight backside against my lap, then apologizing with those big, innocent eyes. Calling me into your dressing room, nothing but a scrap of fabric running between your legs."

"I'm not sorry," she breathed. "You should have given in."

He drew a circle around her right nipple with his index finger, bringing the pink bud to a sharp point. "I held back that night, Lita." His hand closed over her breast, squeezing. "Rough as I was, you *enjoyed* a restrained version of me."

Yes, she did know that now. He'd only allowed her a small glimpse of his dark tastes, hoping to send her running. But it had backfired. Now her curiosity ran neck and neck with unrepentant desire. With the mention of his harsh treatment of her, James's eyes were taking on a faraway look, though. Was he remembering? She needed to keep him here with her, in the moment.

Lita leaned up to bury her nose against his chest, his scent sending her pheromones into a swoon. "You smell so good."

"Yeah?" James scrutinized her, a muscle jumping in his cheek. He clasped her wrists and drew them over her head. Slow, so slow. The higher he placed them, the harder his arousal ground against her center. "Enjoy it now. Because in around an hour, I'm only going to smell like your pussy."

Lita started shaking. James had never spoken to her like that. Even that first night, he'd been so full of visible tension, every command had been issued through his teeth. *Holding back.* This man looming above her was one she trusted, but the nuances, the sudden edge to him excited her beyond words. "I want to smell like you, too."

"Oh, you will."

His hips were so heavy between her legs, creating such sweet pressure. And when he moved them in a rough circle, Lita's eyes rolled back in her head. "Now. *Please*, now. I need you inside me."

"*Goddammit*, Lita." He dropped his head into the crook of her neck on an uneven groan, his hands tightening around her wrists. "Let me fix my mistake."

Right. This was their do-over. His chance to replace his guilt from that night with something good. Something better. With his big body weighing her down into the mattress, his breath rasping in her ear, she was losing focus of that goal. But she couldn't. It was too important. "I'm sorry," she murmured. "You've taken care of my ankle. Fed me...kissed me. What w-would you have done next?"

His stubble slid against her cheek as his head lifted. "First, you'll say out loud what I did to you. I don't want to be let off so easy."

Lita swallowed and focused on the ceiling, her memory calling forth sounds and touches in the dark. "You tied my hands to the headboard…above my head. Then you…"

"Say it."

"You put yourself in my mouth."

He released one of Lita's wrists to tilt her chin up. "That was after. After I made you crawl to me like a beggar, *after* I slapped the hell out of your sweet ass. That's when I propped my knees on the pillows and I fucked your little mouth. Didn't I?" He visibly attempted to center himself but didn't succeed. "You needed a savior and you found Satan, instead. Took you so many times, so many filthy ways in the dark, I lost track. And not once was I gentle. Did I leave anything out?"

Afraid that if she spoke, her words would be incoherent, Lita only shook her head.

Despite the regret he projected, she could see he was turned on. To an immense degree. Could feel his erection bulging against the inside of her thigh. Both of them were panting into the scant space separating them, heating the air. "You liked those things I did to you?"

"*Yes*. My answer isn't going to change." *Goals. You have them.* "The do-over ends at midnight, you know. We just have to make it to midnight and you'll have made up for what happened."

James's frown was thunderous. "You're making this up as we go, aren't you?"

By way of answering, she lifted her legs to surround his waist, loving the way his eyes glazed over. Empowered by it. "I remember how you tasted in my mouth. Your ridges sliding over my tongue. How heavy you are down there."

"I hear your little sucking noises in my sleep. *Fuck*." His hand tightened its grip on her face but loosened as he exhaled. "I've had my turn, though." He released her jaw, coasting his hand down her thigh and hiking up her skirt. "I've apologized to you, now I'm going to repent between your legs."

James's hand cupped her damp flesh, forcing a cry from Lita.

"Mmm. So wet. Does that mean she's in a forgiving mood?" Lita didn't dare answer as James slid his middle finger inside her. Pushed in deep on a low growl. "Yes, she knows. She knows I made sure no one touched. Kept her safe inside those panties, away from hands and mouths that weren't mine."

James dragged his mouth down between her breasts and lower, licking at her belly button twice before settling between her splayed thighs. Lita could barely wrap her mind around the image of James so close to her private flesh. She'd imagined it so many times, but the visual reality—James licking his lips and draping her thighs over his shoulders—almost climaxed her. Illuminated only by the distant bathroom light, he was a dark god, sent down to earth with one intention. To feast and give pleasure.

When he leaned forward and dropped a kiss over her clit, she strained on the bed, hands twisting in the comforter. "Oh, *please*."

He laid another gentle kiss on her flesh. "So, so sorry, little girl." His voice was a thick murmur. "I saw my Lita and got carried away, didn't I? Couldn't handle the way she made me feel. The bad things she made me want to do." He parted her flesh with big fingers and gave a long lick through the middle. "Bad things I still want to do. To her. Only, ever, her."

Lita's thighs attempted to close, but only succeeded in hugging James's head. That single stroke of her clit had already drawn her toward the finish line. So long, she'd waited so *long*. No fair that it could be over so quickly.

"Will your pussy forgive me for being a greedy bastard?" James flicked his tongue over her clit. Fast, too fast. "For not giving her what she deserved?"

"*Yes*," she moaned. "Oh God, I can't *take* it."

"I wasn't finished apologizing."

Before she registered his movement, James rolled over, reversing their position on the bed. It left her straddling his face, her hands clutching at the bedclothes for purchase. "What—" She broke off on a scream when he slipped his tongue inside her, drawing it in and out. "*Ohhh*. Don't stop. *Don't stop*."

The sweet torture lasted a few blissful moments, before he

stopped to tug her clit between his lips. "Now I'm the hungry one, Lita. *Feed* me." He gave her bottom an encouraging pat and she could feel his restraint in the touch, knew he wanted to give her a hard slap instead. After that, she could barely think at all because he stiffened his tongue, a silent command to ride. Lita leaned forward, fists planted above his head. She rolled her lips faster and faster, goaded by masculine hands digging into her backside, propelling, encouraging. The buildup of heat was swift and unforgiving. It sang in her veins like an operatic solo, but her mouth could only repeat *James, James, James.*

He groaned each time she slicked over his waiting tongue, the sound growing louder until it vibrated her clit. Their erotic position, the absolute possession in his eyes, the grip of his hands, her own wheezing breaths…they combined and lifted her past the point of no return. She started to fall forward when the orgasm blasted through her system, but James grabbed her thighs and pressed his mouth closer, *closer,* sucking her clit with such ferocity, another climax wracked her muscles on the heels of the first.

"So good, so good. James. I can't. It's so good."

Finally he released her legs, allowing her to pitch sideways and land on the bed, her body covered in sweat, chest heaving. The skirt was twisted up around her hips, but she didn't have the energy to pull it down. James entered her line of vision, looming above her in the near-darkness. He watched her in that intense manner, that inscrutable stare of his never wavering until her body cooled. His fingers raked up and down her thighs, pausing only when her attention landed on the erection outlined by his jeans. As if he could feel her attention there, his breath turned shallow. "I'll wake you at midnight, Lita."

Something about the way he said the words bothered her, but she didn't pinpoint the reason until the second before sleep claimed her. And she realized what she'd heard in his voice.

Dread.

Chapter Five

James stood beside the motel room's water-stained window, watching the streetlight flicker over the empty parking lot. He could hear Lita's soft breathing coming from the bed behind him. She hadn't shifted once since slumping onto the mattress and passing out, a fact that caused tenderness to build every time he glanced over. Tangled hair lay across her cheek, the way he'd seen it countless times when she woke on the tour bus, but it looked different now. Now, he could put his hands in it. Stroke it. Twist it in a fist.

Damn you. Why couldn't he be content to lie beside her instead of watching the clock, waiting for midnight? Earlier, while cleaning her ankle, he'd noticed chipped pink nail polish on her toes. A detail he should have found endearing, but only made him eager to...corrupt that sweetness. Eager to have those same toes digging into his ass as he pumped and pumped, silencing her screams with his mouth, his hand. All the while, whispering inexcusable things into her ear. Things his rational mind knew were wrong, but his body liked the sound of.

How could he feel such protectiveness for Lita and want to dominate her in such a way? It was as though his two urges went hand in hand. Protect and punish. Cherish and...imprison. Keep her still and make her *take*. He'd never allowed these urges to play out with another woman, because they were only inspired by Lita. When she came into his life, he'd been searching for something without a name. She'd woken up his baser instincts, forced them to take shape, but they'd never gone further than her. Part of him wished it had extended to others, disloyal as that thought made him feel. But at least if this need didn't have a specific target he could walk away. Leave her to a more natural relationship than the one he could provide.

Perhaps when Lita found out about the violence in his blood, she would understand his desires came from a bad place. A place he'd allowed himself to visit in a deconstructed sense the night they met, but was far stronger than she knew. Might even be stronger than *he* knew. His father hadn't merely used his fists on James and his mother. People in town had always given the man wide berth, not knowing what would set him off. Barbeques, town meetings, grocery stores, had all been settings for bloody altercations, incited by James's father.

James had put off college for two years so he could protect a mother who refused to leave, insisting her husband was a good man. During that time, the court had mandated anger management therapy and to everyone's surprise, his father had attended and seen actual results. But James didn't believe in cures. People couldn't change. And that aggression gene had clearly found its way into his DNA.

Lita moved among the bedsheets, curling onto her side. The goddamn skirt was still rucked up around her waist and he'd left it that way, craving the lack of barrier between him and her pussy. The tempting swell of her bottom. His hands could touch if he so chose, a freedom he'd never had before. Her non-concern over being exposed proved how much this girl trusted him. Acting on the images his mind projected could damage that fragile bond, but after four years of denying himself, her invitation was a deathblow to his restraint.

James knew before looking at the clock what it would say. His body had been performing the countdown all on its own. 12:00. A flame, edged with blue, lit beneath the furnace of his body, bringing his blood to a rollicking boil. Jesus Christ, he'd forgotten the drugging rush of power that overflowed when he allowed the dam to give way. If a significant part of him felt like the big bad wolf towering over Goldilocks, his cock rigid in his jeans with the need to defile, *so be it*. He'd tried, he'd fucking *tried*, to leave Lita in peace and she'd shown up, levering green eyes on him, needing him to tend her injuries. Kissing him. Showering for him. Eating for him. Ruining even the tiniest amount of progress.

He couldn't lose himself to the clawing urge, though. Had to remember the last time he'd lost control, how he'd felt afterward. *Keep your head.*

The sound of him lowering his zipper woke Lita. Until she sat up, looking around the room in alarm, James didn't realize the darkness hid him from her eyes. But that realization shot his pulse into overdrive. He held his breath as she eased off the bed and tiptoed toward the bathroom. "James?"

Protector. Corrupter. Which one *was* he? Reassuring words climbed up his throat, while the note of fear called to his animal nature. And he couldn't hold it back anymore. It shouted at him to pounce.

James moved through the darkness, capturing Lita around the waist and spinning her toward a desk situated along the wall. Her muffled scream shattered the room's silence as James pushed her forward, over the surface, using a firm hand to press her cheek down onto the wood. The roar inside him increased in volume when the sexy lines of her body remained taut, full of fight.

"James," she said into the darkness.

"I could very easily be someone else, though. Couldn't I?" Keeping one staying hand at the back of her head, James palmed her upturned bottom. Roughly. Christ, she would be so satisfying to fuck from behind, her little cheeks sliding up his sweaty stomach, just enough space between her thighs to accept the hanging flesh that would swing up and slap her with every drive. She had no clue how many times he'd pictured it, pictured her smart mouth in a round O when she realized he wouldn't be slowing down or easing her in. The way a good man might.

"I-I don't know," Lita whispered and it took James a second to realize she was giving a hesitant answer to his question.

I could very easily be someone else, couldn't I?

His cock swelled through the partial opening he'd created by lowering his zipper, the metal teeth digging into heavy, hungry flesh. Using his forearm to keep Lita stationary, he reached into his pants and freed himself, dropping its weight onto her waiting bottom. She gasped, sending more blood rushing south, thickening him to the point of near agony. God knew he didn't need anything else but the sight of Lita bent over to achieve misery, though. Her palms were flat on the desk, as though grounding herself might keep her calm, when her rapidly rising and falling back told him it wasn't working.

James dragged his erection down the center of her backside, pushing against the separation of her cheeks with a grunt. "It's not smart for such a sweet, young girl to be out after dark by herself, is it? Not so much as a pair of panties to cover you." He rammed his hips forward, his eyes closing over the friction of their flesh, her shaky whimper. "If you cover only one thing late at night, it should be your pussy, little girl. There are hungry men walking the streets, praying someone like you will get brave and venture out, against their daddy's rules."

Lita sucked in a gulp of air, smooth thighs shifting against his hair-covered ones. "I'm...I'm sorry."

His rumbling laughter was unrecognizable to his own ears. "You're nowhere near sorry yet. And I think you know that." James lifted the back of her shirt, licking up the spine he uncovered, his tongue greedy for sustenance. When he reached her nape, he pushed his mouth against the wispy strands of hair, inhaling. "I wonder if I slip a finger into your pussy, would you try to get away from me or just wiggle that pretty ass closer?" He rolled his hips, the head of his cock rubbing against her wet front seam. "Answer me. Are you really the good girl you pretend to be?"

"Yes. I...try to be," she breathed.

Somehow she'd given James the answer he'd needed, when even he hadn't known what it was. His heart jackhammered, loosing his staunchest inhibitions until they were sprinting past undiscovered roadblocks. They were two strangers encountering each other on a deserted street, the darkness giving them an excuse to buck society's dictates and strip down to their basest existence. A tempted male and a coy, breathless female.

Taking another irresistible opportunity to stroke her backside and give it a reproving slap, James let his fingers continue further, testing the damp, addictive heat waiting for him. "Jesus, you're wet all over. Not even fit to be in public, let alone bare-assed in a tight skirt. No bra, either, to keep you decent." With a rough middle finger, he petted her clit. "Know what I think? I think you didn't wear a bra because you want your tits to shake when you walk past a man. Yeah. You were out looking for something. Weren't you?"

She tried to close her thighs around his hand, but he only pushed her stance wider with a foot. "No, I wasn't." A pregnant pause. "Let me go."

On a labored exhale, James's head fell forward into the crook of her neck. Conflict raged within him, two sides of a tarnished coin. And that was *before* she tried to get free. Lita's body jerked, hands reaching behind to shove his body away. The animal she'd uncaged—or maybe they'd done it together—demanded he pin her back down and sink his cock into all that welcoming wetness. Hold her still while he banished the wealth of lust. But he wasn't so far gone that he'd lost sight of Lita. God, he couldn't hurt her again. Not in this lifetime. Even though he couldn't see her face, he could visualize it and could remember how it made his heart pound.

With an astronomical will, James leashed his demons and released Lita, stepping back to give her space. Lungs protesting his lack of oxygen intake, he watched her straighten and face him, cheeks flushed, eyes a little wild, reminding him of that night when she was only nineteen. Fuck, the similarity almost did him in. Made him want to fall at her feet and apologize until the world ended.

"So that's it?" She sauntered toward him, making his eyes narrow. "You're just going to stop?"

"You asked me to stop," he returned through clenched teeth, needing like hell to reach out and touch, grab, overwhelm her.

Closer now—*so* much closer—she raised the shirt over her head, letting it fall to the ground, giving him an unobstructed view of her tits. "I asked you to stop because you wanted me to." She ran her index finger down his abdomen, sending a bolt of need to his still-erect cock, thickening it as she watched. "And because I...*wanted* you to say no."

Yes. The invisible chains holding him back clanked onto the ground. James lunged forward, hauling Lita up against him with one arm, yanking her skirt down with the other. Naked. He wanted her fucking *naked*, without a goddamn stitch to offend him or share access to her body. As soon as the skirt dropped, her legs were around James's waist, the head of his sensitive arousal slipping through her pussy. His hands molded to her bottom, giving her a nice glide up and down an erection that might as well have her name tattooed on it. "You know why you fit me so nice, Lita? Why all I have to do is tilt my hips to go home?"

Her thighs slipped down his sides, so she clung to his shoulders, working to get higher, leg muscles flexing. Even though his hands were braced on her ass, he loosened them a moment and enjoyed watching. Seeing her sexual frustration as she worked to stay on top of his cock. "James."

"Why do you fit me so well?" he grated at her mouth.

"I'm your plaything." Finally having found purchase, she writhed on his lap. "I'm your plaything."

He slapped her backside. "That's right. *Only* mine." God, the flood of lust was battering him from all sides, the need to get inside her fierce. Waiting another second seemed like a travesty, but protecting her came second nature, so he took two steps and set her down on the desk, getting a priceless eyeful of her female flesh as he bent forward the remove his jeans and dig a condom from the pocket.

"No." Lita shook her head. "I don't want that."

His look held a warning. "Lita…"

"*You* brought me to the doctor." Her eyes grew glassy, her slight figure swaying on the desk's surface. "You had me put on the pill yourself. I probably shouldn't find that so hot."

James tossed the condom onto the desk, eased between her thighs and let their mouths graze together. "You tortured me for a week. Blowing kisses to jackass boys in the crowd. Wearing my shirts to bed so they smelled like you the next day." He shook his head. "But I couldn't take chances with you." His knuckle slid over her clit, making her gasp. "Or this."

Doubt crept into her expression. "Is it you, then? You're not-"

He cut her off with his mouth, ending the kiss by rubbing their damp lips together. "In this one way, I'm clean for you." He dropped a hand down to stroke his aching cock. "You want it raw?"

"*Yes*," she whispered.

Somehow, floating in his lust-fueled consciousness was the important reminder that Lita hadn't been with a man in a long time. The testosterone fueling him wanted to take her fast, hard, completely, but he couldn't. Not their first time. "Lita—"

"You're thinking too much." She reached behind him and dug her fingernails into the flesh of his ass, drawing him forward. Their gazes held for a meaningful moment, before she moved her hands to his chest. Smoothed her palms over him in a circle. And *pushed*. "I said, I want to go home."

This time, there was no conflict or hesitation. It couldn't exist when lust, power and need was a vacuum, sucking all the uncertainty free. He wrapped Lita's hair around his fist, hauling her head back and savoring the shocked whimper that passed her lips. "You'll leave when I'm done with you."

When Lita started to struggle in earnest, he released her hair in favor of yanking her hips to the desk's edge. She tried to insert a leg between them, a lever to shove James away, but only succeeded in kicking over a plastic ice bucket and a stack of paper cups. Jesus, the combination of those objects scattering on the floor and her hands pushing at his shoulders made his blood turn thick, made it pound. *Take, take, take.* He allowed himself to experience her resistance, savor it, before wrapping a forearm around her waist and pinning her arched back to the desk.

The position left her thighs wide, her pussy on display. She made a distressed sound, her legs attempting to shoot closed, but he blocked them with his body. He didn't so much as flinch when she slapped his face. "You're not helping your cause."

"Get off of me," she said through her teeth.

James entered her body with a growl, a sound drowned out by her scream. *Christ.* Christ, for a moment, the dark game they were playing didn't exist. He was finally inside Lita and what the hell else mattered? But the tight, sleek feel of her, the hands still attempting to push him away, called to his primitive nature, roused the more intense facets of it. James leaned down, putting his ear directly above her mouth, needing to hear everything that came out. Then he reared back his hips and drove into her hard, closing his eyes at the deafening cry she released.

"Did you ever stop to think about how a man looks…when he's got a woman beneath him?" His voice was a boom of bass in the darkness. "When he's finally got one mounted and spread?"

Her breath feathered his ear. "N-no."

"No?" James slipped free of her perfection and rolled himself forward again, noting how her knees shot high every time he thrust. God, he would love to film that little move so he could replay it for her. Make her *look* at the effect of his plunging cock on her lithe body. "Men were made with this length of flesh that only fits *one* place. Inside a woman. And that flesh gets hard all the fucking time, always aching for that space between a woman's legs. Where it was made to *fit*." He punctuated his final word with a hard thrust, groaning at the way her tits shook. "I'm an animal just like the rest of them. Wanting to get on top of a woman and ride her rough, close my eyes and fuck until the hard flesh we were cursed with doesn't hurt anymore."

Lita renewed her attempts to get free beneath him, ramming the heel of her hand into his pectoral and shifting her hips, heels digging into the desk. All useless movements, despite their vigor. It was dark in the room and her eyes were shadowed, but the dipping of his right shoulder caused light from the bathroom to illuminate her face. Her eyes were glassy but focused on him. Hair a mess, mouth puffy. God, he'd never seen anything sexier in his life. *My Lita.*

Rocked by need and undeniable relief that this experience *with Lita* was far better than some anonymous fantasy, James held her down and bucked his hips, again and again. He was the embodiment of desperate aggression, sliding her body down to meet each thrust, grunting as she sheathed his dick with little cries. Cries that sounded like submission, an offering to the beast harnessed inside him so long. The hands pushing his shoulders were losing their determination, hesitating as if they wanted to tug him closer instead. And James could do nothing but slake his lust.

Just bury his face in her neck and strive with each pistoning thrust to get deeper. *Deeper.* "Oh God, oh God, *oh God...*" Lita moaned into his shoulder, her voice vibrating with the force of his drives.

"Some men are after relief and they don't care who gives it to them," he grated into her neck. "Now imagine a man who only gets hard for *one* woman. Imagine it's a never-ending battle to hide his erect cock because she's *always around.* Giving him little pinkie waves and whining his name, knowing full well what it does to him. I've wanted to fuck you all day, *every* day, since you showed up. *Goddammit,* you little tease."

Lita's hands were on his ass now, their game having shattered apart with his admissions. Head back, mouth open, tits bouncing, she jerked him forward into the promise of relief her body represented. Her knees were hooked under his elbows now, but he couldn't remember getting them there. Couldn't think around the way her wet pussy squeezed him, her husky moans of his name. "Please, James..."

He threw her right leg over his shoulder, freeing his hand to stroke her clit. Damn, her body's reaction to that touch almost choked the seed from his dick, making him pound all the harder into her tightened-up entrance. *Need to come, need to come.* "You put me in so much fucking pain, Lita. Take me out of it." The sounds of their bodies joining filled the darkness. Slaps, strokes, and moans. "Taking it raw, aren't you, plaything? Loving that big, bare cock, aren't you?"

"Yes."

"You want me to coat the inside of you? Fill you full?" His mouth latched onto hers for a slippery, sensual kiss. "Give me yours first."

James pressed his thumb down on her clit and dragged the button of flesh up through her wetness, before letting it go. Doing it again. Her flesh began to shake against his hand, her cries going off like fireworks in a night sky. She fought against him again for a different reason. She was pinned by his thrusting hips, straight through the climax. "Too much." Her fingernails clawed at his neck, his upper back. "*Too much.*"

The pain of her scratching made his release a sharper kind of bliss. He opened his mouth but no sound came out—the pleasure had trapped it all inside. Lita's mouth was his only tether to reality as he shot from the cannon, hanging in the atmosphere as his body weathered a release so complete, it wouldn't allow him to breathe. Just kiss her. Her. *Lita.* Finally, he was forced to rip his mouth away to intake oxygen and Lita was right there with him, gulping in air.

Sweat coated their bodies, but James couldn't deal with being parted from her, so he lifted her limp body into his arms and walked to the bed.

When James laid her down, she dropped a hand onto her lifting and falling belly. "I need…"

Lita trailed off without finishing, making one corner of James's mouth lift. She trusted him to know what she meant, *knew* he would. He returned from the bathroom a minute later with a towel and a glass of water, handing her the drink while he cherished the task of cleaning himself from her body. Thoughts about tomorrow and next week tried to invade the long-needed relative calm in his mind, but he barred them entry. The morning would be soon enough to debate the future. For now, holding a sleeping Lita was the only thought worthy of entertaining. Something he'd needed to do every night for four years, but hadn't allowed himself the privilege.

Looking over her body to reassure himself there were no marks, James laid down behind Lita, pressing his chest to her back. His eyelids drooped—from exhaustion, tenderness, renewed need—when she snuggled closer, fitting her bottom to his groin. "James?"

"Yes."

A small hesitation. "I could really get used to that other side of you."

There it was. That was what scared him.

A horrible twisting took place in his chest.

James didn't sleep that night.

Chapter Six

James had been quiet all morning, but Lita wasn't fazed. She *knew* this man well. With James, brooding was just par for the course. Not to mention? Hot as shit.

His Broodiness sat in the driver's seat, once again in a pair of faded jeans, this time with a fitted, white T-shirt that hugged his biceps. A hint of his boxer briefs was visible around the waistband of his pants and she wanted to lick the entire perimeter until he begged for her to go lower. Yeah. After James had given her the Orgasm To End All Orgasms last night, Lita wanted a one-way ticket back to bed. She wanted to be roughed up and held down. Wanted more of his disrespectful words issued beside her ear. And she wanted it now.

Unfortunately, James had already been fully dressed when he woke her up by opening the window blinds in a loud *zip*. Thanks to the haziness of sleep, she'd made a clumsy attempt at seduction by fluffing her hair and winking. He'd left the room like wolves were on his heels, saying he would wait in the car while she got ready.

"You forgot about the rule," Lita said, donning her Ray-Bans.

"Which rule is that?"

Wowee. Had his voice always rumbled like that? It blew cool air across her senses, creating goose bumps in its wake. She could hear it saying *plaything* in the darkness. "Uh, you know. The one. Never wake a musician before noon."

His lips twitched. "That rule only applies on the tour." He slid a glance—not his first—across the car's console to where Lita's legs were crossed. Maybe she was playing dirty with the cut-off jean shorts, but hey, it was a hot day outside. She totally got away with it. Although, she really hoped *James* didn't let her get away with it.

The only way for her plan to succeed was persistence. And after last night, after she'd gotten to the bottom of his fears, her new goal was…a relationship. One that didn't have secrets or hidden insecurities. One where they could be themselves without being afraid of hurting one another. If she'd approached the situation with James with any sort of rational thought earlier, instead of acting out, they might have gotten to this point sooner. Instead, she'd damaged his trust. Now she would make up for it by handing over hers. *I trust you. I trust you.* If she proved those words through her actions, he would start to believe it. He had to, right? The alternative was going back to Los Angeles without James and the very possibility of that reality…honestly, it terrified her to think about.

"Remember that time I woke up Sarge with a water balloon?"

Lita had to catch her breath when James gave a rare smile. "Oh, I remember. He slept with one eye open for a month."

"Hid my sticks as payback, too. Right before a show, the bum." They coasted to a stop at a red light. "I kept expecting him to balloon me back while I was asleep, so I kept one loaded underneath my bunk." She shook her head. "The attack that never came."

James drummed his fingers on the steering wheel. "Oh, he tried. I stopped him."

Lita frowned. "Why?"

Silence passed while he pulled through the intersection. "I didn't want anyone to see you sleeping. They weren't allowed in the back of the tour bus."

A low pulse started just south of Lita's belly button. "Is that why you were always the one to come wake me?" James said nothing, jaw flexing as he watched the road. Lita wasn't letting it go, though. "Did you always want to get in bed with me?"

"*Every. Time.*"

Lita's nipples hardened inside her bra. "I would have welcomed you," she breathed, reaching over to trace the waistband of his jeans with her index finger. "I used to touch myself thinking about it. You slipping into my bed when everyone was asleep. That big hand covering my mouth to keep me quiet so no one would hear."

"*Jesus*, Lita." He adjusted himself with a strangled groan. "We're not talking about this now. I have a meeting in ten minutes."

"A meeting?"

"Yes. An important one." His gaze pinned her back against the seat. "You wouldn't be wearing clothes right now unless I had a good goddamn reason."

"Oh. Point made." She rolled down her window, allowing the breeze to cool her heated face. "Who is your meeting with?"

His voice was strained upon answering. "A realtor."

Lita shot forward in the passenger seat, pressure already beginning to burn behind her eyelids. "Why? You're not...m-moving here. *James.*"

"No," he said quickly, shooting her a worried look. "No, my parents moved into an apartment closer to town. My mother asked for help selling the house."

Lita tried not to be obvious with her relief, but slumping down into the seat like her puppet strings had been cut probably gave it away. With her heart so firmly lodged in her throat, it took her a few minutes to speak again. "Is this the house where you grew up?"

"It is."

Pleasure washed away the remaining tension. Coming to Modesto had been the best decision she ever made. Or maybe just the first good one. Not only was she making headway with President Broody, she would actually get a peek into his past. Until that moment, she hadn't realized how starved she was for information about where he'd come from. What events had brought him to her that night in the hotel bar?

"Don't get too excited. The house is empty," James said, breaking into her elated and somewhat sappy thoughts. "Anyway, I haven't been back here in a decade. It's been even longer since I lived in the house."

James slowed the car and turned into a small, blacktop

driveway. It was empty, signaling the realtor hadn't arrived yet. Lita was too busy focusing on him to notice much else, though. "Why haven't you been back?"

"My father and I aren't on good terms." He turned off the car's ignition. "I'm here to help sell the house and run the business for a while. That's it."

Lita made no move to get out. "Tell me why you don't speak to him."

He opened his mouth but closed it just as fast. "Another time, Lita."

While Lita attempted to swallow the hurt, James climbed out of the car and rounded to her side. He opened the door and helped her out, eyes and fingers lingering on skin far longer than was necessary. James's way of apologizing for shutting her out? Probably. But she needed to be patient instead of pushing.

Feeling the burn of James's regard, Lita turned her attention toward the house. "Wow," she laughed. There were flowers. Everywhere. A million different colors, all vibrant. Lush greenery and tall, leafy trees surrounded the small, cottage-style house, making it look like something out of a fairytale. "This is not what I pictured at all," she said, climbing the porch stairs. "Maybe I should have when you told me they owned a landscaping company."

James passed her on the stairs, keys in hand. "Yes, it has always been pretty on the outside."

Wondering at his cryptic statement, but determined to keep the morning light, Lita followed James into the house. White walls and dark wood floors greeted her, but the paintjob was obviously fresh. Not a single trace of the family who had lived there before. "Show me your room."

"It's not my—" He broke off with a sigh. "It's upstairs."

Lita preceded him up the creaking steps, imagining photographs lining the walls at one point. Homey smells coming from the kitchen downstairs. All the things she'd missed out on growing up. "Which way?"

"To the right."

Based on his husky tone of voice, James was looking at her backside. Lita smothered a laugh as she turned the corner and breezed in through the only open door. The bedroom was small, but bright; empty, save the fluttering blue curtains blowing in front of the open windows. Lita faced James, refusing to dim her enthusiasm one notch. "You slept right here for eighteen years."

"Why does that make you smile?" he murmured.

Lita executed an awkward pirouette at the room's center. "Because you just showed up one day, like you'd come into the world fully formed as an adult. You know *everything* about me, witnessed my best and worst days..." She stopped turning and shrugged. "So I have one thing now. I have one, and maybe in another four years, I'll have two..."

Transfixed by his intense expression, Lita trailed off, her ability to speak deserting her. James came forward, although *barreling down on her* was a more apt description. Long, determined strides that kept her rooted to the spot, sending her heart into a fit of erratic beats. His mouth swooped down onto hers and opened, pushing her lips wide. On a simultaneous groan, their heads tilted opposite directions, mouths interlocking like the final piece of a jigsaw. *Oh...oh God.* She could barely stand under the assault of *feeling*. Drugging, dirty, fucked-up passion that made her white blood cells *scream* and she couldn't get enough. Couldn't *ever*. Lita's hands tangled in James's hair the same time he walked them backward, giving Lita the wall to lean on while he mouth-fucked her.

Holy shit. The seam of her jean shorts was damp within thirty seconds of James stroking his talented tongue along hers, again and again, hungry sounds ripping from his throat. His hands slid up her outer thighs and gripped the frayed ends of her shorts. "I will destroy these before the day ends."

"They're kind of already destroyed," she panted. "It's a look."

His laugh emerged on a puff of air, stirring the hair he'd messed up in his hands. A beat passed as he scrutinized her face. "I played water polo when I was younger. There's your second thing, all right?"

Lita's mouth dropped open. "Did you wear a Speedo?"

"Hmmm. A white one."

Two very potent emotions were fighting for precedence— hope, because he'd opened up to her, even with such a small thing, and all out *arousal*, because his powerful body had her plastered up against a wall, his pupils dilated enough to obscure the gray, *need* like she'd never seen in their depths. "James?"

He dipped his head to suck at her top lip, slowly pulling it into his mouth and letting it go. "Yes?"

...aaand arousal won the day. Lita wedged her right hand between their bodies and gently squeezed the bulge behind his fly, running her fingers over the thick outline until she found the plump tip. *So big. God, he's so big.* "I need to get on my knees for you. For this."

"*Fuck yes.*" James placed his hands on the wall, easing his hips back to give her room to work the button and fly of his jeans. "I'm going to bang your beautiful mouth, Lita. Just the way you like it."

She nodded, unable to catch her breath. "Yes. Please."

Even though James hadn't lived in the house in ages, there was still something illicit about unzipping his jeans and fisting his erection, giving it a slow pump as she exposed him completely. His hips rolled in time with her strokes, mimicking sex. Only with James, it wasn't mere sex, it was giving in to compressed need. His teeth were bared, the veins in his biceps growing more prominent. A man that could break her and didn't mind making that clear.

Lita dropped to her knees, wrists crossed at the small of her back. She couldn't say what intuition drove her to that position, only that it was what James would like. What *she* would like. His arousal was delicious fruit inches from her mouth and she couldn't stop staring, wanting to taste him, pleasure him.

Before Lita could lean forward and take his flesh between her starving lips, James threaded his fingers through her hair, tilting back her head. "Ah, Lita." His fingers tightened around the strands. "I would kill a man for doing the things I want to do to you."

"*Hello? Anyone up there?*"

Lita waded through the cresting surf of desire to pinpoint where a third voice had come from. Downstairs. A woman. Realtor. "Ohhh."

"Goddammit." Pain clear in his features, James hauled Lita to her feet, holding her steady as she swayed. "You look at me...you smile, and I forget everything."

Oh. Oh wow. "Really?"

Gaze narrowing, he paused in the crucial act of stowing his still-erect manhood back inside his jeans. "Yeah. Really."

"I wish I could be sorry," she said, more than a little breathless. "So...after you meet with the cockblock downstairs, can we go back to the motel?"

He zipped his jeans with a wince. "Later. We have work to do first."

"Work?"

On the way out of the room, James threw a wink over his shoulder. "I hope you're ready to get dirty."

"I don't think we're on the same dirty page," she called after him, unable to banish her smile. Playful James? She could get used to that.

Chapter Seven

This was getting out of hand.

Twenty yards away, Lita was bent forward on hands and knees, digging with a hand shovel in the dirt. It was a good goddamn thing he'd sent the rest of their landscaping crew to another section of the property to work, because anyone seeing that hot, young backside swaying in the air but him? Not. Happening. The men had already shown way too much interest upon arrival, asking for pictures and autographs when recognition dawned.

James had a lot of experience steeling himself against the urge to scoop Lita up and carry her away when men spoke to her on the road, their familiarity with her persona making them way too chummy. So he'd gritted his teeth and gotten through ten minutes of listening to Lita charm the crew out of their fucking minds before sending them far away as possible.

They worked outside a newly built commercial space surrounded by a wooded area. He was supposed to be uprooting a rotted tree stump, but nothing could keep his eyes off the little white strands of frayed denim ticking the underside of her ass cheeks. Every time she exerted pressure on the ground with her hands, her back arched, allowing his gaze to follow the denim seam where it ran down the middle of her pussy. Every so often she would sit back on her heels and stretch, tightening the tank top's material across her tits, lifting it to expose her stomach.

His hard cock was lodged between the waistband of his jeans

and his abdomen. His balls ached with the need to empty. Visions of Lita on her knees like a sacrifice wouldn't leave him alone.

So why was James enjoying himself so much?

Maybe because they were…talking. Not the usual way they spoke to one another, taunts and warnings issued like cannon blasts. This was different. His secrets were out on the table now. And damn if her plan to replace their first night together with something better—something he could be proud of—hadn't worked. The guilt that typically sat in cactus form inside his chest was less spiked today. The compulsion to apologize every time they locked eyes had eased. While he still had major reservations about dragging her into the dark fog inhabiting his brain, spending time with her was an aphrodisiac. He craved having her close. Watching her expressions change. Listening to her unique logic.

God, she was something.

"So you were on the water polo team." She sent him a sly look. "I bet you were beating the chicks off with a stick."

He wiped the sweat off his upper lip. "You think I'm going to answer that?"

She went back to digging with a half smile on her mouth. *That. Fucking. Mouth.* "Did you have a nickname?" Wanting to hear what she would inevitably come up with, James stayed quiet. "I bet they called you the Torpedo in a Speedo."

James laughed under his breath. "Nothing as good as Lita Bandita."

"I'm *still* mad that didn't stick," she said, throwing down her shovel. "You cause one little panic…"

"You fired blanks during a show and started a stampede for the exits."

"And you cleaned it up for me." She shifted on her knees. "You always cleaned it up. I should have said thank you more."

"Don't worry about it." He wiped his dirt-streaked palms down the thighs of his jeans. Jesus, he couldn't handle her acting sweet. If she'd been in reaching distance at that moment, she would have been on her back. "Old News is going back into the studio in a month," James prompted, cursing himself for bringing up a sore subject. As it stood, he wouldn't be in the studio with them.

"Yeah." She dragged the tip of her shovel back and forth through the dirt. "It might be good to rehearse once or twice beforehand, right? It's going to take the Jaws of Life to pry Sergeant from Jasmine and the new house."

His throat started to ache. "What about you? Don't you eventually want a house?"

Her laughter sounded forced. "I don't know. Do houses come with room service?" They fell silent for a few minutes until she spoke again. "An apartment, I think. A two bedroom so I have a place for my kit. Maybe a balcony in case I feel like some late-night bungee jumping."

"Lita…" James warned.

She turned sparkling green eyes on him, but there was a hint of sadness in them that made him miserable. "There we are."

James wanted to erase the last five minutes and start over. Go back to when they were teasing each other and she was prodding him for information about his younger days. It had felt so good. Then he'd fucked it up by reminding her he'd left the manager position behind. She was just playing defense by putting them back on more familiar ground of wayward drummer and killjoy.

Had he changed his mind about leaving Old News with a new manager? Since Lita had arrived dripping blood, his focus had been zeroed in on her. The sexual hum that followed them everywhere. Time had come to face facts, though. Before she'd followed him to Modesto, there had been zero chance of James severing all ties. He'd resigned himself to checking up on Lita through the new manager. Now? Now she'd shown up with the obvious goal of shooting down each and every one of his reservations. And Jesus, it was working. She didn't think he was a monster. She…liked his aggression in bed. Encouraged it.

Could he let her go back to Los Angeles alone? Go on tour without him there to keep her protected? Just thinking about it made his skin feel like ice, even beneath the blazing sun. Still, there was a relentless prickle at the base of his spine. A doubt he'd been harboring since he'd woken up four years ago and seen the discoloration of her fading bruises.

Maybe she liked men like him. Men with violence in their

blood. An unhealthy fascination that he would be taking advantage of.

James watched Lita as she dug much harder than before, her frustration with him and their conversation plain. Dirt flew to one side, filtering in through tall grass. He was familiar with this side of her. This shaken Coke can of emotion she turned into right before acting out. Doing something reckless. Usually, it put James on high alert, forced him to play offense before she could make a move. But it was a different Lita that had shown up in Modesto—Lita the planner, the fighter—and he couldn't read her as well now.

He started toward her, but drew up short when the crew of workmen rounded the building. Five sets of eyes that landed on Lita without delay, widened with appreciation of her position on hands and knees. Feeling his control begin to strain, James cleared his throat loudly until they gave him their attention.

Only one of them had the decency to look ashamed. "Uh. Lunch time, boss?"

"Yeah," James growled, watching Lita come to her feet. This was it. This was when she flirted with other men or exposed more skin to make him insane. He'd shaken the Coke can and now it would explode all over him.

"You want to come with us, Lita?" the apparent mouthpiece for the crew asked. "There's a decent food truck back toward the main road. Plenty of room."

Lita smiled innocently at James and it was a punch straight in the gut. He hoped she could read the warning in his no bullshit expression. Hell would be frozen over before she got into a car with five men he'd known just over a week. If she wanted a scene, he would damn well give her one.

"Thanks, but no thanks," Lita said to the men. "I'm good here."

James barely managed to hide his shock as the men disappeared from sight. They stared at one another across the expanse of green until the sound of vehicles pulling away could be heard in the distance.

"I'm going for a walk." Lita took off the gardening gloves covering her hands and tossed them onto the ground before reaching up to loosen her hair where it had been kept in a ponytail since they'd started working. It fell in messy waves around her shoulders and she pushed impatient fingers through the strands to tame it, but the movement had the opposite effect on his body. Her jean shorts slipped down onto slender hips, leaving a thin gap between her stomach and the denim. A place for his tongue. His hands. All the while, she glared at him. "Don't follow me."

James felt his blood go from simmer to boil, felt the weight of lust settle low in his abdomen, spreading down to his loins. His hands shook at his sides until he fisted them. Oblivious to the change taking place inside him, Lita turned on a booted heel and stomped toward the wooden area, those little strands of frayed denim taunting him as her ass worked side to side. His dick grew thick and ready for the spot between her legs. He fucking *craved* her. There was no reason among the chaos. Just knowledge that others had wanted Lita, regardless if she'd turned them down. They'd still looked and coveted. Now she was angry and he wanted that anger beneath him. Wanted to harness it, tame it, mate it with his own.

When she turned at the forest edge to flash her middle finger at him, James put his head down and moved. His strides covered ground quickly, but Lita clearly had other ideas. James was about ten feet away when she turned and ran full speed in the opposite direction.

His vision flickered.

* * * *

Being pissed off and horny at the same time was a deadly combination.

Oh, Lita was fuming as she ran along the shaded dirt path. James thought she was so predictable, did he? Thought she was some walking cliché who needed to resort to jealousy to score points? Well, screw the hell out of that. They were way beyond petty jealousy at this point.

The way he'd looked at her like some wayward teenager, even after she'd come here to make things right burned. *And* it had come right on the heels of him so casually reminding her Old News would be continuing on without him. God, maybe this whole trip had been a waste of her time. He'd made up his decision and the longer she spent here, attempting to change his steel-trap mind, she became more of a fool.

"*Lita.*"

She ran faster, her footsteps falling in time with her scattered breathing. Her jagged heartbeat. Plans had gone out the window and now instinct ruled the day. He'd made her feel like the weakest version of herself and now she wanted to return the favor. Or...*God*, maybe this was a last-ditch effort to break through to him. She didn't know anymore. Could only run away from the idea of living without him. Run away from the girl that had driven him away, the girl James believed her to be.

Tears obscured her vision but she pushed on, ducking off the path and sprinting across a forest floor of soft, brown earth and green, fallen leaves—

Lita's progress came to an abrupt halt as her feet left the ground. An unyielding arm banded around her waist, yanking her backward into a chest that left no doubt her captor was James. She could smell his singular musk, she could...feel his excitement against her bottom. The evidence that her impulsive run had yielded that effect somehow incited her rage, while still managing to swamp her in arousal.

"*Stop.*" James rasped the agonized word into her neck but negated the command by thrusting his erection against her backside.

A part of Lita wanted to turn and soothe him, take away the misery she could hear in his voice. But she wouldn't. If he was determined to send her home a failure, she'd prove a point first. This thing that had kept them apart so long, this facet of him that he didn't think she could handle? She'd been game for it since day one.

"Stop what?" She tried to pull away, but James hauled her back. "I'm not running anymore. You won't *let* me."

His groan lifted goose bumps on every inch of her skin. "Lita, I'm in trouble here. Say the words."

"Which ones? Fuck you?" She pulled her elbow forward and

rammed it back into his stomach, satisfied when his vile curse burned her ear. It loosened his hold long enough for her to pull free and start running—only to be brought down to the forest floor, flat onto her stomach, James's grip circling her right ankle.

Yes. Yes. Oh my God, yes. Hot, pulsing anticipation began to trip and skitter through Lita's veins, racing below her belly button, bursting like fireworks. She clawed at the dirt in an attempt to get away, but being prevented, being pulled backward through the damp dirt to the space beneath James's hungry body almost blinded her with hunger. She wanted to be forced down and taken. Wanted her body used without apology. Hard.

Now. *Now.*

She also didn't want to ask. She wanted to be *told.* It wasn't merely the dark brand of lust, but anger and frustration at the man pinning her down. If he wanted it, there was no way in hell she'd give him permission. Her pride wouldn't allow it.

"Get off me," Lita said through clenched teeth, attempting to twist onto her back and being thwarted. "I *hate* you."

"Not yet." He transferred his weight to one side, creating room to run his palm up the bare back of her thighs, where he fingered the fringe of her jean shorts. "But you will if you don't say the goddamn words."

That grating command gave her a burst of energy. Lita threw an elbow back and connected with his collarbone. Nothing. He didn't so much as flinch. Was he made of granite? Even without seeing his face, she could imagine the tense lines between his eyebrows. Could see brackets around his sensual mouth. Feel the starvation pouring off him in waves. His touch moved higher to palm her bottom, separating her cheeks and squeezing them crudely.

Wetness trickled down between her thighs, forcing her to swallow a gasp.

"We talked about this, Lita." His tone had changed, grown more predatory, and everything inside her sung in response. "We talked about that tight cradle between your legs and how well I was made to fit there. You've been flashing it at me all morning like a dick tease."

"No, I haven't," she breathed, knowing full well it was a lie but liking the way it felt wrong on her tongue. Loved the way wrong suddenly felt right. Vital.

"A liar, too, aren't you?" He crammed his hand between Lita's pelvis and the soft ground, working the button of her pants with ruthless movements. Every nudge of his knuckle against her belly set off a chain of sparks inside her. Bright, needy sparks. "What am I going to do with this hard cock, Lita? How am I going to satisfy myself unless I fuck you into the ground?"

Her zipper came down with a muffled, metallic sound. Big, blunt fingers invaded her panties, stroking through her wet folds without a hint of gentleness. The first contact of skin on skin paralyzed her in its long-awaited perfection, but his middle finger's rough jostling of her clit woke her limbs up. It stung in a brutally fantastic way. A way that would bring an orgasm tearing through her middle without consent, and she couldn't allow that. Not a chance. Not yet.

Lita slammed her thighs together and attempted to crawl away on her elbows, crying out in surprise when James pounced on top of her. Not with his entire weight, but enough that she had no chance of freedom. That fact didn't stop her from struggling, bucking up into his immovable hips with her backside. His arm wrapped around her upper half, putting his forearm beneath her mouth, so she bit him. *Bit* him until he repositioned them with a threatening growl and captured her jaw. Lita was a total prisoner now and it caused shivering thrills to race from the tip of her head downward, curling her toes. *Yes. Don't let me move. Keep me.*

"What are you fighting me for, plaything?" He rasped into her ear. "You've been asking me for this all morning. 'Come and get it, James.'" His hips rolled against her bottom. "I heard you even if you weren't saying it. I can hear you *now*."

"No." *Yes. I've been begging.* "I didn't ask...I don't—"

Lita's protest died when the jean shorts were yanked down her body, along with her panties. Her lips fell open to suck in frantic breaths. They were outside doing this. Her pants were down, exposing her. *Outside.* And she wanted what would come next so bad, her fingers curled into the dirt, grinding the grains against her palms and creating abrasions. The same way *she* wanted to be marked. Claimed. Corrupted. *Now, please, now.*

Their bodies were so close, the back of his hand grazed her bare backside as his zipper was brought down. When he heaved a groan, she knew he'd removed his erect flesh, could picture its ruddy girth clasped in his hand. The way he stroked its length above her imprisoned body. Looking down on her. Preparing to *take.*

Using what felt like his knee, James shoved her thighs apart, dragging her wider knees in the damp earth. "Next time you'll think twice about heading into the woods alone. Won't you, little girl?"

A whimper tumbled from her mouth. Depending on who was listening, the sound might have been distress or arousal. Her thighs could have been shaking out of fear or anticipation. She could barely keep up the pretense of non-consent anymore. Another minute and she would be screaming for him to get inside her.

She felt the fleshy head of James's arousal slide through her core, pausing at her entrance. "Oh God, oh God..." she chanted, voice cracking.

James jerked her hips up, leaving her bottom in the air, her cheek pressed against the ground. "He can't help you, either."

When he seated himself inside her body, it took Lita's scream a few seconds to work free of her throat, oxygen was at such a premium. Even when the piercing cry finally found its way into the air, James's hand cut it off after only a few seconds. Her vision wavered under the attack of his body on hers. No quarter was given. No mercy. He was a hostile man determined to use her body as an outlet for lust. His hips dipped down and rammed up in forceful thrusts that jarred her teeth inside her skull. Without the brawny arm supporting her midsection, keeping her center in place for the taking, she would have fallen flat.

Inside her mind, a vision of James interchanged with a shadowy stranger. One he'd kept locked inside. A side that came out and turned him into a different man. But that blurry juxtaposition of trust and uncertainty only made it real. Made her the only thing standing between this man and relief from his pain. There was power in that knowledge, even with her body held immobile.

James slowed his movements and leaned forward to align their bodies, chest to back, as he teased her with slow, thorough drives. "Put you on the pill to protect you, didn't I? From who?" He uncovered her mouth and hammered into her with a series of rough thrusts. "From *who*?"

"*You*," she shouted.

"That's right." He rose again, gripping her hips as their bodies joined, again and again. "All that acting out and getting into trouble. Maybe you just needed to flash that pussy at me and run away, somewhere I could make you sorry and no one could hear you scream."

Irritation flickered in Lita's chest, traveling down through her arms. She didn't like hearing that her efforts had been wasted. That he'd managed to maintain control around her for so long while she'd been suffering. Memories of those nights tossing and turning in her bed, wishing for James, hardened the muscles in her legs with frustration and she pushed, shoving backward. Simply to show she still could. That he hadn't won yet. "*Asshole.*"

James's hardness slipped from her body with a grunt, but he remained upright on his knees, his grip a touch looser on her hips. Enough for her to turn around and slap him across the face.

Lita's back hit the ground a second later, adding to her shock that she'd struck him. James loomed above her to block out the filtered sunlight, pinning both wrists above her head and wedging his sweating body between her thighs. Concern swirled in the gray of his eyes, but not enough to block out the animal need there. No, his desire was visible and rampant, much like the flesh hanging between his thighs. "You *know* how to make me stop. And that's not it."

She ached to scream the words, just so he'd *have* to stop. Just so he'd have *some* idea of the pain she'd been in living without him. Knowing she might be required to do it again. But if he stopped, she would ache from now until her dying breath, would regret it with every cell in her body. She *needed* him. So she clamped her lips shut and fought to free her wrists, knowing full well he'd never let go.

But then, he *did*.

He freed her wrists.

It was so unexpected, her hands fell backward to frame her head. "What—"

James dropped down to interlock their lips, scrutinizing her as they breathed into one another's mouths "You don't really want me to stop." Their lips slipped together in a sensual mating dance. "Do you? Lita?"

The touch of dread in his deep voice undid her. Before she could think of a response, Lita's heart answered for her. "No." She shook her head back and forth in the dirt. "Never."

Before the word fully escaped her mouth, James entered her once more on an agonized groan, his mouth finding the side of her neck, sucking and biting as he started to move. His first few drives were even, controlled, but the drag of his stiffness over her clit drove Lita a little crazy. *More. More.* She clawed at his ass, arching her back, until she felt the now-familiar snap in his surrounding energy. Both of her knees were hooked beneath his arms immediately—and then he fucked her into the ground. Just as he'd said he would.

Teeth sunk into available flesh, fingers dug into muscle, hips collided, clothes were torn. Lita didn't recognize the sounds coming from either of their mouths. They were desperate and foreign and often angry.

Their coupling turned rough. Violent. The lust for danger had built too long and now it took over, urging Lita to issue whispered challenges to James. Sometimes daring him to go harder, sometimes begging without shame. Those dares made him bare his teeth, picking up her body just to pin it back down with breath-stealing force, his bottom half never ceasing, pumping relentlessly.

"You little brat. I should have started fucking you a long time ago. Maybe you'd have some goddamn manners by now." He shoved a forearm beneath her ass, lifting her lower body up to his lap to receive him. "Or maybe I just bought myself four years of relative sanity. I'm going to lose a little more of my mind every time you slip down onto my cock, aren't I? Every time you *breathe*."

Lita was teetering on the edge of something catastrophic. Air wheezed in and out of her lungs. Her leg muscles started to freeze up. The angle of James's thrusts prodded a spot inside her that rendered her unable to form words, lest she disturb the brutal accuracy. Shit, *shit*...she couldn't orgasm like this or she'd break apart into nothing. Too much—too—

Stars blinded Lita as the crisis powered through her lower body, clenching her every muscle in a way that made her instantaneously sore. Her scream sounded distant, like someone had turned down the volume on a movie. James covered her mouth with his own, meshing their bodies together as he rode out his climax above her, his masculine roar of relief muted against her lips. It wouldn't end, ripples and shocks of pleasure spreading, a boulder dropped into a still pond. Her heels dug into the small of his back, her body writhing in the disturbed earth.

"James, James...I'm...I *can't*."

Her world tilted when James scooped her off the ground, cradling her on his lap and squeezing the limited amount of oxygen from her chest. "I've got you. I've always got you." His lips skated over her features, lingering on her forehead. "Please, tell me you're okay, Lita."

There was no veiling the truth after what they'd done. Only trust. At some point since venturing into the woods, her anger and doubt had evaporated. She'd needed *this*. Craved *this* exchange of trust. It's what she'd needed from James all along. What they'd needed from each other. "I don't think I've ever felt better." She laughed when her words were a little slurred. "What about you?"

When James didn't answer right away, she tilted her head back and saw she hadn't managed to convince him. His attention raced over her skin, lighting on her ripped T-shirt, the bite mark on her shoulder, the smeared dirt...everywhere. His jaw looked tight enough to shatter. "Hey." He wouldn't meet her eyes.

No. Fuck this.

She'd never felt closer to another human being in her life than she did right now. He wasn't going to drift away on her. Lita scrambled to face him fully, throwing her legs around his hips and framing his face with her hands. "Kiss me and you'll know that everything is going to be fine."

There was only the barest hesitation before James broke,

devouring her mouth with a gruff sound. In between kisses, he rasped words of apology, praise, amazement, worry.

"Didn't hurt my gorgeous girl. She's still here with me. I'm sorry I was a prick. God, I've never felt or seen or touched anything like you. Mine. *My* Lita."

She absorbed it like a greedy sponge, letting him cut off her oxygen with his banded arms and smother her in whisker-burn kisses. It was the single greatest moment of her life. Having James call her his girl in the woods, her body depleted and their skin pressed together. She wanted to build a cabin in that very spot and live there forever.

"We need to get back," James muttered into her hair. "I can't let anyone see you like this."

"Fine. Okay." She swayed as he pulled her up, onto her feet. "Look how agreeable I'm being."

"Don't make a habit out of it." His gaze heated as it roamed over her legs. "I like when you fight me."

Whoa. Lita's knees wobbled. "I like the way you get even," she breathed.

For one lightheaded moment, Lita was positive he would tackle her once again to the forest floor, his expression was so ravenous. Instead, he growled a curse and took her hand, leading her back the way they'd come. She didn't even bother containing her smile as she stumbled along behind him, not sparing a single care about her disheveled state.

Until they walked into the clearing and came face to face with half a dozen police officers, red and blue lights flashing behind them.

Chapter Eight

James shoved Lita behind his back, positive he'd been transplanted into the middle of his own personal nightmare. Or maybe the universe was balancing out the heaven he'd just visited by casting him into hell. It couldn't be reality. But it was. He could feel Lita's hands sliding up and down his back, could hear her whispering into the material of his T-shirt, words that wouldn't penetrate the denial revolving like a hurricane in his brain, throwing debris in every direction, intent on destruction.

"We received reports of screams coming from the woods."

A silence followed the officer's statement, the brief but heavy kind that ensues after a hospital patient flatlines. He'd heard that kind of silence before. Coming from his mother when the police showed up at their house, shuffling their shiny shoes on the porch. Police that may as well be identical to these men, attempting to stare straight through him to Lita. To ascertain the damage they'd already glimpsed. And what had they seen? A woman who'd been mistreated. A woman with marks on her body, inflicted by a man. Him.

We received reports of a disturbance coming from the house.

How many times had he heard those words growing up? Except now, he wasn't comforting his mother in the living room while his father "got rid of" the cops. No, he *was*...his father. He was the monster hiding the damage. Guarding his own victim. God, he was nothing but a self-fulfilling prophecy.

Lita's hand started to shake inside his, and he automatically tightened his grip. Protecting her came before anything else. Or it *had* at one time. They were facing a veritable firing squad and her only armor was a ripped tank top and mud-stained shorts. As far as he was concerned, he'd just forfeited his right to protect her ever again. As a lover, friend, or manager. He'd failed her three different ways.

And Jesus, if he'd just walked away four years ago, he'd have only failed her in one way. As a human being. *Selfish.* He'd been too fucking selfish. One last time, he would allow himself to play protector. Just one.

"I'll answer any questions you have, but I need to get her into my car first."

The officers traded what they probably thought was a covert glance. It wasn't. They were weighing his demeanor, the tension in his voice. Determining whether or not he was a threat. They were right to do it. "We're going to need to speak with her, too."

Lita pulled on the back of his T-shirt. "Let me talk to them. Come on, it's just a misunderstanding."

James turned his head slightly but didn't meet her eyes. "Is it?"

Her hand dropped from his shirt.

The back of James's neck pulled tight. How dare he feel so possessive of her? A shout threatened to burst from his throat, commanding the officers to stay away, knowing damn well the command should come in reverse. He should stay away. But rationality where Lita was concerned had never been his strength. "She'll talk to one of you. Not all six."

Ignoring the pain in his chest, James gripped the hem of his T-shirt and ripped it over his head, handing the garment over his shoulder to Lita and leaving himself bare-chested. For a moment, the shirt remained suspended in air before she moved, pulling it over her head. Covering herself.

This was why he'd maintained rigid control for four years. This is what happened when you gave the wrongness inside you an inch. It took a mile. No. He wouldn't displace responsibility. *He'd* taken a mile. And now Lita would pay in the form of embarrassment. Judgment.

When James realized the officers were staring down at his uncovered chest, he wondered if the gaping wound in his heart was visible, but upon further inspection he saw what had drawn their notice. A slash of red, angry nail marks decorated his chest. He didn't even recall her scratching him.

"Aren't you Malcolm Brandon's son?"

That question sounded as if it had come from inside the blue and red flashing lights, but when the asker came forward to reveal himself, James recognized the officer right away. The same officer who'd stood on his porch all those years ago, summoned by their neighbors. *We received reports of a disturbance coming from the house.* Only this time it was James, not Malcolm. The condemnation and disgust in the officer's eyes was a bullet straight to the gut.

It was obvious that James's father's name rang a bell for each of the men. Eyebrows went up. Not just in recognition but in speculation. *Like father like son.*

James's momentary shock gave Lita her opportunity to stomp past him. "Hiya, boys. Sorry you came all the way out here for nothing." Her laughter echoed in the silence, but James could only focus on the desperation in her voice. "We got a little carried away while hiking. That's all."

"Lita." James stepped forward to take her arm but drew his hand back when one of the officers laid a hand on his gun.

"*Jesus.*" She shoved a clump of dirt-streaked hair behind her ear. "Don't tell me this is the first time someone messed around in the goddamn forest around here."

Uncomfortable shifting among the officers. "All due respect, ma'am, none of them walked out looking like you." That came from the same man who'd questioned his father countless times. "Do you need medical assistance?"

"No. *No.*" She buried her face in her hands. "Oh my God. This isn't happening."

James couldn't see her in distress another second. He stepped forward and blocked her from view once again, painfully aware that he'd just performed the same maneuver Malcolm used to pull. "You heard her."

Another round of pointed looks among the officers. One

reached into his pocket and removed a business card, coming just close enough to hand it over to Lita. "We'd appreciate if you'd give us a call later. Let us know how you're getting on, would you?" The officer turned his attention to James. "Tell Malcolm we said hello."

It seemed like an hour had passed when the last officer had climbed into their police vehicle and left the site, each minute creating more distance between himself and Lita, destroying him a little more. When they were alone, Lita stormed toward his Mustang without uttering a word, climbing into the passenger side and slamming the door.

James walked slowly toward his execution, even though *he himself* would be the one to deliver it. He'd also set himself up for it. Living and breathing Lita for so long, knowing it could come to this if he lost hold of the reins. *Red and blue flashing lights. Pitying eyes all over Lita. God, what had he done?*

Before he'd even shut the driver's side door, Lita launched a grenade at him across the console. "Please, let's just laugh this off. Okay? Let's go home and laugh about that time we got caught red-handed by some jerk-off cops." Her voice rose to a plaintive tone he'd never heard out of her mouth. *"Please?"*

James had to close his eyes against the urge to drag her across the car, rock her back and forth in his lap. "Those cops were just doing their job, Lita." His stomach lining thinned, burned away by the rising acid. The secrets he couldn't hold onto any longer. "Same way they always did their job coming to our house to question my father. When he couldn't keep his fists to himself."

He could sense Lita's scrutiny, but the sensation cut off when she slumped back in the seat. "So that's what all that cryptic man talk was about, huh?" A long pause wherein he could hear her swallow, hear the wheels turning in her beautiful head. "Your father…hit your mother."

It hadn't been a question so James remained silent.

"Is that why you don't speak with him?"

He nodded once. "It wasn't always the neighbors that called the cops. Sometimes it was me. Until I got old enough to stop him myself." They exchanged a knowing look. "After that, cops were no longer necessary."

Lita remained the stillest he'd ever seen her. "I'm sorry you went through that. I'm sorry for your mother, too."

"Because you understand what it's like."

She didn't quite flinch, but her smooth skin turned pink as if she'd been slapped. "Stop trying to bait me. I know where this is going. You think you've turned into your father. You think you're repeating the pattern." Her left hand unfolded between them on the seat as if she were begging him to take it. Hold it. No. It would never end if he held her hand. It would give him a comfort he didn't deserve. A reprieve from the oncoming blow. Still, her hand stayed there, taunting him. "I'm telling you that's bullshit, James. *Listen* to me."

James picked a spot on the dashboard and trained his eyes there, refusing to look at Lita. "I listen to every word you say. I hear you in my goddamn sleep."

"Same," she breathed, scooting a little closer and breaking his already hemorrhaging heart. "What we do together is nothing like what your father did. Nothing. You have to realize that."

He swallowed the temptation to believe her. It would be so easy, but they'd be back here tomorrow. And the day after. He'd push further every time and eventually she'd break. So he'd break their connection first. For her. *Everything* for her. "It is the same, Lita. You just can't see it." Somehow he found the will to face her, look her square in the eye. "You can't see it because this is your normal. You think *I'm* your normal. You seek out men like me."

She recoiled. "Excuse me?"

"You had...bruises when we met. You came from an ugly household, just like me, and you landed right in the midst of another. Now you've found a third in me." Oh Jesus, her face. Her face crumbled and James wanted to die a thousand deaths, but he pushed on out of sheer will and necessity. "I'm not the only one following a pattern, Lita."

She inhaled in a huge sob. "Oh, fuck you, James. Just fuck you."

The words—the hurt and betrayal in them—dug into his chest like fired bullets. "I'm sorry, I know—"

Her palm cracked across his face, the sound breaking like

thunder in the car. For long beats, their accelerated breathing was all that tempered the silence. "Why aren't you hitting me back? Huh?"

"Lita—"

"*No.*" Her voice shook. "No, you've made your point, now you'll listen to me. I left my parents at seventeen to escape a bad situation. I left. I *survived.* And I left again when my boyfriend hit me. Survived. *Again.* You don't get to call me a victim. How *dare* you." She pressed a closed fist to her mouth a moment. "The difference between my ex and you is... I consented to what we do. Not what happened before. I thought there was love behind what you and I were doing. Or the...hope of love. But I guess I was wrong. Because you must hate me to call me a willing victim to my face when I've done nothing to deserve it."

Panic crept in slowly at first, but it began to storm, pelting him in doubt at denial. "You misunderstood me. People can be strong and still make mistakes—"

"Oh, own it. *Own* what you said." She shoved open the passenger side door. "You better because you're losing me over it."

It took James a second to react when Lita jumped out of the Mustang and stormed toward the road. He followed suit, her words replaying in his head like a broken record. Had he read the situation wrong? He'd never considered any of it from her point of view. Survivor. Not victim. "Where are you going? *Stop.*"

"You don't get to know where I'm going anymore," Lita shouted over her shoulder before she halted and turned on a booted heel. She got right in his face, backhanding him with her raging beauty. "I only packed enough clothes for three days. Did you know that? I thought...I love James. And he loves me. And we can figure this shit out in three days." Her head fell back on a hollow laugh. "You need longer, though, to pull your shit together. A lot longer."

I love James. I love James, she'd said. Lita started to walk away again, but reflex had his hand shooting out to capture her elbow. "Just give me a minute to think, will you? I thought I understood all of this and I just need to *think.*"

"Yeah, so do I." Her green eyes turned sad. "We need to do it without each other around, though. I'm going back to Los Angeles."

His stomach rebelled. "Christ, I don't want that."

She shook her head, sending two tears falling down her cheeks. "Right now, I don't care what you want."

It didn't matter if he deserved that, it felt like a death blow. "You just told me you love me. How am I supposed to let you leave?"

"Same way I watched you leave, I guess," she said, the words ending on a sob. His knees threatened to collapse. God, he'd been a fool. Hurt his girl. Hurt her so bad. Needing to hold her, he reached out, but she evaded him, stumbling a little on the grass. "If you figure this out, James…if you work your way through this belief that your love is bad for me, you know where I'll be. But don't come find me unless you're ready. Please." She clutched at her chest. "I can't take any more."

Smothered in disbelief, James watched the love of his life—the reason for his existence—walk away, farther and farther from him. How had this happened? He'd expected a sense of relief, rightness, over having set her free. But the doubt over what he'd done was battering him from the inside. A voice berated him from the back of his mind, telling him he'd been wrong. So very fucking wrong. He'd hurt her far worse with his words than he ever could with his body. "*Lita*," James shouted, striding after her. "Please don't leave. Come back here and kiss me. Know that everything is going to be fine."

Lita paused. "Too late for that," she said without turning around. And kept walking. Leaving James standing on the road, invisible blood pooling around his feet.

Chapter Nine

When Lita returned from Modesto, Los Angeles looked different. As if she were seeing the traffic, the sidewalk cafés, and tourists through a new pair of eyes. For so long, life had been about making it to the next moment. Riling up James. Buying new drum equipment. Sleeping off the crazy night before. Ignoring the pain every time James refused to *see* her. Touch her.

No more, though. She was done. It was time to stop waiting for wishes to come true, for other people to handle her decisions and start doing for herself. If there was an added benefit of keeping her mind occupied, instead of focusing on the slashed-to-ribbons organ stuttering inside her chest, well...the distractions didn't hurt either.

She spent her first night back in Los Angeles packing her hotel room. No more rock star purgatory for Lita. Her packing style of throwing everything into giant boxes from Staples might have been messy and unorthodox, but it got the job done. Next, she found a real estate leasing agent online and viewed several two-bedroom apartments before settling on a bright, airy duplex in Santa Monica, not too far from the beach. She sat there now, cross-legged in the empty living room, going through her wallet to scrutinize the credit cards.

Had she applied for any of them—or had it all been James? And holy shit, it hurt to think about him. Great, gulping breaths accompanied any mental recitation of his name, as if the very thought of his presence sucked the air from the room. What was he doing? Would he ever come back? The uncertainty heaped on top of her like dirt being shoveled from a grave. Maybe she shouldn't want him to return to Los Angeles. After all, the credit cards and various memberships spread out around her on the floor proved he'd taken up too much space in her life.

Not all his fault, though. Not all. She'd leaned on James, loved him taking care of her needs. She'd craved it because it was the only way he'd shown affection for four years. The only tangible proof that he felt something.

He'd felt something, all right. Pity. He hadn't taken care of her out of love, he'd done it out of guilt. Over their first encounter. Over wanting to play rough with a girl he didn't think was mentally healthy enough to handle it. If she was being fair, her actions over the course of four years did nothing to prove his theory wrong. She'd been reckless, acting out at every opportunity. Perhaps it had been wrong to assume he could see beneath the surface to the strength beneath. Perhaps it had been naïve to think her trip to Modesto would show him in such a short space of time that she wasn't *just* an unruly brat. She was a woman that loved him and hadn't known how to express it, because she didn't know what it looked like.

Until he'd shown her in his own way, among the trees, before tearing the ground out from beneath her.

Lita stared at the cards for long moments before rising to her feet and digging a pair of orange-handled scissors from the kitchen's junk drawer. She sat back down on the floor and cut up the cards, snipping them in half, one by one. No more relying on other people for her needs. This was her life and she would take control. Starting now.

Ignoring the tears that blurred her vision, she dialed the bank to make an appointment to close her accounts and open new ones.

* * * *

James stared back at his reflection in the rearview mirror of his Mustang, wondering when he'd had time to grow a full beard.

Although, time had become an irrelevant detail, hadn't it? He showed up to places when he got there. Plans and schedules and punctuality were all laughable parts of a past life. The very notion of planning *anything* when his thoughts were so fucking occupied was impossible. He couldn't think around the knowledge that Lita was somewhere hurting. And he was the cause. He'd been the cause for a very long time and making plans that didn't include her felt like hurting her all over again, whether it made sense to his exhausted mind or not.

Since she'd walked away a little over a month ago, he'd worked. His father's manager had shown back up to reclaim his position, but James hadn't been ready to give up the distraction that was physical labor. So he'd taken on a co-managerial position that allowed him to take his frustration out on hard earth, day in and day out. Just as he'd done with Old News, James had found new avenues of success for the landscaping company, taking on eight new commercial contracts in the space of four weeks, allowing them to bring on new staff. Buy new equipment.

Distractions. All of them.

Distractions from the fact that he'd been wrong about Lita. He'd mistaken her inner strength for a weakness. She'd overcome huge obstacles in her life and he'd downplayed them, made them a pattern of which he'd become a part. Inexcusable. Her expression of horror and disappointment when she realized he'd underestimated her...it was the first thing he saw upon waking, if he managed to sleep at all. Most of the time, he didn't. He lay awake, staring at the motel room ceiling, replaying their relationship since the very beginning.

At present, he'd made it to year two. The year Lita attempted to crack him with an extreme sports binge. Bungee jumping, cliff diving, racing lessons. He'd been a wreck for months, not sleeping for worry she'd sneak behind his back and attempt some stunt before he could verify it was secure. At the time, he'd been livid with Lita. Lecturing her nonstop. Using his authority to keep her out of harm's way as much as possible. Now, James wished he could go back to those moments. Go back to having Lita parked on the tour bus bumper in front of him, belligerence in every line of her body…and tell her she was amazing.

That's what she'd been trying to tell him, right? Show him? That she was resilient and unafraid. Daring and strong. While James had only seen someone hell-bent on harming themselves. How he could miss Lita's message when he only ever looked at her baffled James. God, he'd been blind.

Well, he wasn't now. And there was no way to come back from calling a woman like Lita weak. No way to repair four years' worth of damage. He'd done the worst of it inside that very Mustang, could still feel the ghost of her sadness in the passenger seat, haunting him.

James shut off the ignition and stepped out of the car, into the hospital parking lot. His father was being released tomorrow and enough was enough. He'd respected the man's wishes not to visit since arriving in town, but James's resolve not to go after Lita was taking a rapid nosedive. He missed her like fucking hell. Missed her wit. Her cocky smile. And now he knew what she felt like beneath him, knew the bliss of being inside her. So going to her and begging until his face turned blue had become seriously appealing, especially since his return to Los Angeles was imminent. In order to prevent himself from going straight to her doorstep, he needed to go look his father in the face. And see himself reflecting back. James needed a reminder that Lita had a better future than one with a man like him.

A man who needed too much control. A man who needed to dominate her in an extreme way to get off. A man with violence in his blood. Lita might believe she loved him, but as he'd proven with his misjudgment, he wasn't worthy of love that forgiving. He wasn't worthy of a woman so strong when he couldn't even overcome his own weaknesses.

James strode through the sliding glass hospital doors and walked straight into the waiting elevator. Since he'd been handling the insurance paperwork for his mother, he knew exactly where to find Malcolm Brandon in recovery. When he walked into the dimly lit room, one would have thought his father had been expecting him for the lack of surprise on his face. Malcolm had aged a lot, although since James hadn't seen him in so long, it wasn't apparent how much the stroke had to do with Malcolm's pallid skin, new wrinkles. But his father's eyes were exactly the same as he remembered. Steady and calculating.

"I don't want to see you."

James leaned against the far wall and crossed his arms. "Yeah? That's too damn bad."

Malcolm snorted. "Still not afraid of me." At once, his father looked weary, his head flopping back against the pillows. "You never were."

"No." James waited for his father to start shouting, waited for his hands to fist in the bedclothes. To transform into the man of his memory. "I'm going back to Los Angeles tonight. I just needed to know some things before I went."

After a heavy moment, his father waved a hand. *Go ahead.*

It took James a while to formulate exactly what he needed to say. He hadn't walked in with a plan, only knew that he couldn't let the opportunity to learn more about himself pass. "How did you stop?" He paced to the window without taking his attention from his father. "How did you learn to control the...violence?"

Malcolm's face twisted. "What is this?"

"Just answer the question."

His father's shock faded in degrees. "I stopped feeling sorry for myself." James hadn't been expecting that answer at all, but Malcolm pushed on before he could question him. "Not all of us excel at whatever we set our minds to. Look at you, waltzing in here from Los Angeles and increasing my profit margins in the space of a month. Fifteen years ago, I would have hated you for that. Because I couldn't do it. Still can't do it." The older man rubbed at the gray stubble dotting his jaw. "I would've felt how...smug you were. Even if you weren't smug at all. And I would've felt the rage build and build at you, at myself. Until it took me over."

A pushing started behind James's eyes, someone prodding him with a fork from inside his head. This wasn't what he'd expected at all. Wasn't how he'd envisioned this conversation going. He'd expected to relate to his father on some unsettling level, but none of what Malcolm said sounded remotely familiar.

"It always went back to me feeling...less than. And it took me a lot of years to admit that." He encompassed the room with a sweeping gesture. "I still feel less than once in a while. Why do you think I didn't want you to see me like this?"

James stared out the window but saw nothing. "I thought you were still upset over all those times I called the police. Or what came after. The fighting."

"No. You did the right thing." James turned to his father, saw his face was a mask of shame. "Thank God your mother forgave me or I'd have nothing."

The fork behind James's eyes twisted, visions of Lita's smiling face in the forest dancing in his head. "So the violence…it was always about you. Not the person you focused it on?"

The older man's swallow was audible. "James, sometimes I forgot who I was even fighting and only saw myself."

Was it possible that he'd not only underestimated Lita…but himself, too? Never once had his urges been about harming Lita. Jesus. *Never*. His needs were driven only by giving her pleasure. Satisfying his darker tastes *with* her. Not using them *against* her. God, he'd even sensed she needed the same rough satisfaction he did. Perhaps she'd been the very thing that called his baser instincts to the surface.

No, not perhaps. Lita *had* been the catalyst, all those nights ago in that meat market bar. He'd not only spent the last four years denying his own needs, but *hers* as well. And that… *That* was unacceptable.

Every moment that passed without her was a crime. His stomach turned over and pulled, just imagining her miles away, alone, being her brave, irrepressible self without him. She didn't need him. Her walking away had proven that. But James needed her to live, to breathe, to function. Needed her close.

Could he convince her to trust him again? How?

When the answer came to him, he was already halfway to Los Angeles.

Chapter Ten

Lita adjusted her headphones and closed her eyes, testing the drumsticks' weight in her hands. Usually, that electric silence coming through the headphones before they started recording was chock-full of anticipation. Excitement. A high that couldn't be explained to a non-musician. Sarge called it the Magic Minute and it was where he usually turned around and made some goofy face at her, guitar at the ready. He might even be doing it while she sat there, poised on her throne, but she couldn't check because her eyes were stuck closed. She didn't want to open them and see a stranger at the engineering desk.

Until now, the day they would begin recording the new album, Lita had been wearing blinders regarding the new manager. *He would show up.* She'd actually *believed* James would show up today. That he would be standing there, patient and sturdy, in the studio. That he would give her that classic James nod that meant, *right, let's get the show on the road.* But he wasn't there. He'd let her walk away and now? Now she would record her first album without his level gaze keeping her centered from behind the glass. And her heart was splintering and cracking all over again, sending little pieces of timber dropping into her stomach.

Tears she'd managed to avoid for weeks were poised, hot and ready to fall, so she reached into her back pocket and ripped her sunglasses free, shoving them onto her face. Her bandmates were watching her out of concern—and rightly so. They all needed to be on top of their game when recording. This morning, she'd woken up so sure she could handle this—and she would—she *would*.

Thirty seconds left until they started.

Lita exhaled slowly toward the ceiling.

"Lita." Sarge's voice invaded her ears. "You good to go?"

She nodded. She shook her head. She nodded again.

"We can stop," said the lead singer. "Pick it up tomorrow."

"No." Her foot slipped and hit the bass drum pedal, making a low boom inside everyone's headphones. "I'm fine. I'm fine."

I'm not fine. I want James. I want him here. Why doesn't he need me back? I hate him for not needing me back. But I love him so much.

The new manager's light, feminine tone replaced the voice in her head. "We can take five, Lita, but we're on a schedule. We need to lay this track today."

Lita swiped her wrist under her nose. "I said I'm ready. I don't need five."

When her voice cracked on the final word, a silence filled with skepticism ensued. She gripped the drumsticks so hard, the bones in her fingers protested, pain bloomed and spread up her forearms. Oh God, she'd done so well until now. She'd bought furniture for her duplex. Decorated the shit out of that motherfucker. She'd been the one to schedule band rehearsals, even providing wake-up calls to their lazy bass player when necessary. All her accounts had been transferred into her name. She'd been paying bills on time without fail. There had been temptation to fly off the handle and do something reckless in the hopes of bringing James back, but she'd resisted.

But this…this was *so much harder*. She and James had started this band together, put it together piece by piece. They'd been here first, never acknowledging out loud that James's intention had been to create something for *her*. A chance to do what she loved. All of it for her. But now she was abandoned and maybe, just maybe, she didn't want any of it without James.

"Lita."

Her rioting emotions screeched to a halt, then picked up at one hundred times their original speed, tearing through her blood stream like a horse race. She opened her eyes, afraid to draw breath in case she'd imagined James's voice coming from the other side of the glass. But no, he was there. Bearded and dressed down. *He was there*. Familiar and different, all at once. She wanted to drop her sticks and run toward the booth. She also wanted to throw them at the glass. Unable to decide, she could only look down, rolling her stick against the high tom-tom. "We're trying to record an album here. What do you want?"

Electric silence. "Is that what you're doing? It looked more like stalling." He reached up to adjust his tie, but he was wearing a T-shirt and that stupid, nothing movement almost choked her with love. "You're the best drummer I've ever seen. So what do I want? I want you to stop moping and act like it."

Lita yanked off her sunglasses, irritation needling her from all sides. Odd, though, there was something else beneath the layer of *I-want-to-kill-him*. It filled her with helium, making her weightless. "Take a seat and watch how it's done," she said directly into the microphone hanging over the kit, tossing aside her sunglasses.

"I'll stand."

She ground her teeth and gave the engineer her signal that they were beginning before giving the countdown. Just before they launched into the track, she caught Sarge's smile, but everything but James was peripheral. He *was* the music. Always had been. She'd lost her love for it before they met, forgot she could be good at something, and he'd brought it all back in. Just as he was doing now.

As Lita wailed on the drums, leaning forward during the chorus to lend her vocals, she felt him inside every downward movement of her arms, every vibration of the bass in her stomach. Toward the end, her throat started to ache. Swallowing became difficult. She could feel James watching, watching, as always. His confidence surrounded her, lifting her off the ground. *You're the best drummer I've ever seen*. He'd never said that to her before. Others had, but she'd only ever wanted to hear it from him. Because he never said anything he didn't mean. Just like he'd meant everything he'd said in the car.

That reminder came just as the song ended. Lita let the sticks drop to her sides, winded, gaze locked on James through the glass.

Her instincts screamed at her to run to him, jump into his arms and ask questions later. That was why he was here, right? Looking at her as if he might expire if they didn't touch soon? But she stayed put. Waiting for what? She didn't know. Only knew it better be fucking good.

James leaned forward, mouth hovering over the microphone a second before he spoke. "Lita, I don't know how much time I have. But I need you to know…" he shook his head. "I *live* for you. You're not just in my thoughts, you *are* my thoughts. Every single one. And somehow, I lived for you all wrong. I should have been living *with* you. Not only *for*." His hand gripped the microphone. "I should have seen how capable you were and known we were always in this together. I'm sorry. I'm…sorry doesn't really cover it. Because you're crying and I wish I was dead seeing that. Fuck, I really do. But I already died when you left."

Lita swiped the back of her hand across her cheeks, dashing away the rolling moisture. His explanation was necessary, but God help her, as soon as he'd said *I live for you*, any remaining resolve had broken. But her legs weren't moving, weren't allowing her to travel his direction. Relief and love and surprise had weakened her knees. "What do you m-mean, you don't know how much time you have?"

James threw a glance at the door but didn't answer her question. "I love you, Lita. Even if my mistakes made it so you can't take me back, I'll always be somewhere, loving you with every single thought. Every memory I have stored up." Even though everyone in the studio could hear him, it felt as if only she and James were present. "My first memory of you is that brave, determined girl in the bar. I don't know how I forgot. I don't know—"

Adrenaline found its way to her heart, jumpstarting the organ along with her legs. Lita jumped from her throne, leaping over wires and sprinting full speed toward the sound booth. She caught just a hint of James's relieved expression through the glass before the door swung open and she tumbled through. James scooped her up before she'd set foot inside the room, burying his face in the crook of her neck and chanting her name in a gruff voice.

"I lost you. I *lost* you."

She wrapped her legs around his hips and clung, treasuring every frantic kiss of his lips up and down her neck. "You found me, too," she whispered. "Twice now."

He pulled away just enough to press their foreheads together. "There's no excuse for what I said. I was *wrong*, Lita." The words floated over her lips. "I'm protective over you because I remember living without you. I remember the *waiting*, even though I didn't know that's what I was doing. And when you finally appeared, I took protecting you too far. You didn't need protecting. You needed me. We needed each other."

Her heart couldn't take any more. It pounded in her chest like the bass drum during a wicked solo, erratic and powerful. "Do we have each other now?"

James groaned against her mouth. "Lita, bring me back to life. Tell me you actually want me after everything I've done."

"Of course I do," she sobbed. "I don't know how to stop wanting you. Wanting you is part of me. I like it right where it is."

His kiss was one of cherishment. "I love you."

Tears fell down Lita's cheeks. "I love you back."

She leaned in to kiss him again, but a commotion behind her in the studio caused James's body to stiffen. His gaze was full of regret, but there was a hint of something else she didn't recognize at first. But slowly it dawned on her. Mischief? She'd never seen James house mischief in any shape or form. It had to be a mistake.

"What's going on?"

Footsteps sounded on the floor behind Lita, coming in their direction. "I had a backup plan, in case you weren't ready to listen yet." He kissed her one final time, then set her down. "So I hope you have bail money. Because I might have stolen a police car and drove it here."

Lita's mouth dropped open as two officers skirted past and pulled James's hands behind his back, slapping handcuffs on his wrists. "James. I...what..." she sputtered. "You could have been killed. Do you know how much danger you put yourself in?"

His gray eyes were the lightest she'd ever seen them. Light and focused on her. As always. "It was worth it to see your face right now."

"I've never been more turned on in my life."

Ignoring the officers' reluctant laughter, James stroked her with a head-to-toe look. "Excellent timing."

"I'll be right behind you with bail." Lita pressed both palms to his cheeks and went up on her toes to speak against his mouth. "James?"

"Yes?"

"Kiss me and know that everything is going to be fine."

He did. And it was.

Forever.

Epilogue

Two months later

James let himself into Lita's apartment and carefully closed the door behind him. The sharp sounds of her drumming sailed down the stairs, forcing his heartbeat into the rhythm she created. He knew the song, knew the section she was working on.

Perks of being the band manager.

However, he much preferred the perks of being Lita's boyfriend, which included having keys to her apartment. Along with permission to come and go without consulting her. To take her by surprise when she least expected it.

James wouldn't even attempt lying to himself. He wanted to live with Lita. Whether it was here in the apartment or at his house ten minutes away, he wanted to live his life immersed in every goddamn facet of her. The way she woke up like a cat, rubbing her cheek on the pillow and purring in her throat. How she only ever drank one sip of coffee, then switched to orange juice. The pride she took in the apartment and the personalization of her space. He didn't want to take that away from her any time soon, so he contented himself with spending the night as often as possible, without taking away from what she'd accomplished on her own.

After returning, he'd questioned his desire to continue as band manager for Old News, wondering if he should leave Lita to rule the professional part of her life, but she'd been horrified at the idea of him not returning. And in the spirit of being honest with himself, the idea of Lita traveling around the world without him? It didn't sit well, to put it mildly.

As James climbed the stairs, Lita started the drumming section over, improvement noticeable with each run-through. Practice time was about to be over, though. James was starved out of his fucking mind for his girlfriend...and his intentions were the furthest thing from pretty. They were dark, dirty, and urgent. Just the way Lita liked them. Not that she would tell him that until after. Oh no.

Over the last two months, James had been beyond relieved to discover he found the same overwhelming pleasure making love to Lita that he did playing rough. It was just a different type of pleasure. Smooth instead of coarse. Sweet instead of razor-sharp. Every time their bodies were joined, his soul threatened to burst free, no matter how or when or where.

But today...today his urges were dealing in specifics.

He stopped in the doorway of Lita's second bedroom, his gaze tracing the line of her neck, the toned muscles of her back as she played the drums. Christ, how had he managed to keep her? Her beauty couldn't be described and it only increased with every passing day. He knew that for a fact because he never stopped looking at her. Couldn't force himself to look away.

The amazing part being...Lita was usually looking right back at him. They'd started a tradition of sorts, when James's old worries crept up after a particularly hard session in bed. When he looked at her disheveled state and wondered if he'd been right before. That he was bad for her. Not that she allowed his thoughts to get far, usually climbing on him and making him talk. Express his worries out loud. Their tradition had started with him, during that empty month in the Modesto motel room when he thought living without Lita was his only option. When his memories of her were the only thing keeping him sane. Now, he shared them *with* Lita. He recounted things she'd done and forgotten about, but of which he remembered every detail. That time she'd bought parachute pants and given the entire band, including him, the silent treatment for laughing. That time she'd skinned her knee stage diving so badly it needed stiches and he'd carried her a mile to the hospital because the fans were blocking the road and thus, the ambulance. The way she'd cried into his chest the whole way, breaking his heart in half. That time she'd bought him a bow tie for Christmas that squirted water, and he'd actually worn it with a straight face. The way she'd looked so pleased he'd almost broken down and kissed the life out of her.

Now, James narrowed his eyes on Lita. Had she shivered? Or was that his imagination? Secure in the music disguising any noises he would make, James lowered the zipper of his jeans and gave his growing cock room to extend. Knowing what would come next, a tremor moved through his hands before they went steady. Still and ready.

When he reached over to flip off the overhead light, a cut-off scream from Lita found his ears. "Who's ther—"

His hand clamped over her mouth. He dragged her off the stool, knocking it onto its side in the process. She kicked and twisted, struggling to get free, but James held fast, grunting when her heel connected with a shin. "Who's there?" He spun her around, pushing her body back against the closest wall. "The man who fits, little girl. That's who."

James settled his open mouth against her neck's pulse, licking the unruly flutter. Both of her wrists were manacled in one hand and pinned over her head, freeing the other to reach beneath her skirt and divest her of underwear with a tearing sound. Having her pussy bare always made her kick up a fuss and this time was no different, her body bucking and writhing, an unwilling prisoner. The force of her struggle sent her hips bouncing off the wall, right back into his, where his cock waited for the contact. "Stop." she whimpered. *"Please."*

His mouth raked over her cleavage as he fisted his dick. "Save some of that begging for when you really need it." He dragged the head of his erection through her slick folds before surging up in one savage move to fill Lita, her piercing scream ringing in his ears. "Now. Now would be a good time to beg."

"Please. *No.*"

Releasing her bound limbs, James jerked Lita's knees up around his hips and took her screaming against the wall, gritting his teeth against the smarting pain of her slapping hands...the dark satisfaction that followed in short order when she stopped resisting and her body began undulating in time with his merciless drives. Her moaning and wetness and sweat and *fuck*. All of her. *Everything*.

"You fight me, but your body needs punishing, doesn't it? *You love it*." He cupped her bottom, parting her cheeks in an attempt to get even deeper. "You love *me*?"

Her nod was uneven, green eyes glassy, but fierce. "Yes. Yes." She clung to his shoulders as her body started to shudder. "*I love you*."

James followed her over the edge. "I love you, too. *God*, I love you so much."

Minutes later, the perspiration cooling on their bodies, James gathered Lita close as possible on the bed and whispered another memory into her ear. About the time he watched her eat chocolate donuts. How she'd looked so brave.

THE END

Sign up for the 1001 Dark Nights Newsletter
and be entered to win a Tiffany Key necklace.

There's a contest every month!

Go to www.1001DarkNights.com to subscribe.

As a bonus, all subscribers will receive a free
1001 Dark Nights story
The First Night
by Lexi Blake & M.J. Rose

Turn the page for a full list of the
1001 Dark Nights fabulous novellas...

Discover 1001 Dark Nights Collection Three

HIDDEN INK by Carrie Ann Ryan
A Montgomery Ink Novella

BLOOD ON THE BAYOU by Heather Graham
A Cafferty & Quinn Novella

SEARCHING FOR MINE by Jennifer Probst
A Searching For Novella

DANCE OF DESIRE by Christopher Rice

ROUGH RHYTHM by Tessa Bailey
A Made In Jersey Novella

DEVOTED by Lexi Blake
A Masters and Mercenaries Novella

Z by Larissa Ione
A Demonica Underworld Novella

FALLING UNDER YOU by Laurelin Paige
A Fixed Trilogy Novella

EASY FOR KEEPS by Kristen Proby
A Boudreaux Novella

UNCHAINED by Elisabeth Naughton
An Eternal Guardians Novella

HARD TO SERVE by Laura Kaye
A Hard Ink Novella

DRAGON FEVER by Donna Grant
A Dark Kings Novella

KAYDEN/SIMON by Alexandra Ivy/Laura Wright
A Bayou Heat Novella

STRUNG UP by Lorelei James
A Blacktop Cowboys® Novella

MIDNIGHT UNTAMED by Lara Adrian
A Midnight Breed Novella

TRICKED by Rebecca Zanetti
A Dark Protectors Novella

DIRTY WICKED by Shayla Black
A Wicked Lovers Novella

A SEDUCTIVE INVITATION by Lauren Blakely
A Seductive Nights New York Novella

SWEET SURRENDER by Liliana Hart
A MacKenzie Family Novella

For more information, visit www.1001DarkNights.com.

Discover 1001 Dark Nights Collection One

For more information, visit www.1001DarkNights.com.

Discover 1001 Dark Nights Collection Two

About Tessa Bailey

Tessa Bailey is originally from Carlsbad, California. The day after high school graduation, she packed her yearbook, ripped jeans and laptop, driving cross-country to New York City in under four days. Her most valuable life experiences were learned thereafter while waitressing at K-Dees, a Manhattan pub owned by her uncle. Inside those four walls, she met her husband, best friend and discovered the magic of classic rock, managing to put herself through Kingsborough Community College and the English program at Pace University at the same time. Several stunted attempts to enter the work force as a journalist followed, but romance writing continued to demand her attention. She now lives in Long Island, New York with her husband of eight years and four-year-old daughter. Although she is severely sleep-deprived, she is incredibly happy to be living her dream of writing about people falling in love.

Thrown Down
(Made in Jersey #2)
By Tessa Bailey
Coming April 4, 2016

He has one last chance to deserve the girl of his dreams...

Overachiever River Purcell was never supposed to be a struggling single mom, working double shifts just to make ends meet. Nor was she supposed to be abandoned by her high school sweetheart, breaking her heart into a thousand jagged pieces. Now Vaughn De Matteo is back in town, his sights set on her...and River is in danger of drowning a second time.

No one believed Hook's resident bad boy was good enough for River. Not even Vaughn himself. But he'll fight like hell to win back the woman he never stopped loving, to keep the daughter he never expected, and convince himself he's worth their love in the process—even if he has to rely on their fierce and undeniable sexual chemistry.

But even as River's body arches under his hungered touch, the demons of the past lurk in the shadows. Waiting for Vaughn to repeat his mistakes one last time...

* * * *

"How much longer?"

Vaughn De Matteo groaned the words into River Purcell's sweaty neck. This was it. His life was over. Or beginning. Fuck if he knew. His world had been whittled down to one incredible fact. The girl he'd been in love with since time began—or so it seemed—was beneath him in a rucked up prom dress.

And she was minutes from turning eighteen.

"I…" The breathy music of her voice warmed his ear. "The clock s-says two more minu—" She broke off on a cry when Vaughn got pumping again, thrusting his abused cock up against the lace barrier of her panties, creaking the motel room bed springs. Christ. They'd been at this for an hour. Vaughn getting worked up and River soothing him back down. To wait.

"Who did you dance with dressed like this?" His voice had gone hoarse, scraped, tortured. "You look like some kind of fairy."

"Only because I knew I'd see you afterward," River whispered, pushing back the hair that fell into his face. "I don't dress up for anyone else."

Vaughn's laugh sounded agonized as he dragged his forehead down the center of River's body. Through her cleavage, down the labored flutter of her belly button, stopping at the source of his baser lust, his frustration. River's pussy. And he hated himself for calling it such a vulgar name when those crucial minutes hadn't ticked past yet, but Vaughn reasoned he'd earned that liberty by refusing to fuck his younger girlfriend for two painful years.

"One more minute, Vaughn."

He exhaled a curse between her legs. "You dress up for me, huh? The no good prick who can't afford nothin' but a cheap place that rents by the hour?" After finally securing one of the condoms he'd brought around his hurting flesh, Vaughn curled his hands around River's risen knees, unable to stop his lips from gliding over the swath of pink lace. "Ah, God. You sure you want this, doll?"

River's fingers tugged at his hair, urging him back up her body. "You're the stubborn one who made us wait. I've wanted nothing but this since my sophomore year. Nothing but you." With those blue eyes shining up at him, those unbelievable words hanging in the air, Vaughn couldn't have refrained from kissing River if world peace depended on it. How'd I get this lucky? I shouldn't have gotten this lucky. Senior class presidents from educated families don't date thieving dropouts with no future. No one had clued her in?

When Vaughn finally managed to tear himself away from the frantic kiss, she surprised him by dropping the pink panties onto the bed beside them. "Time's up."

He cupped his girl's cheeks, careful not to abrade her skin with the roughness of his palms. "I love you so damn bad, River Purcell."

"I love you, too." Her voice was unsteady, her fingers tunneling in his hair. "I'll never, ever stop."

Vaughn double-checked the digital bedside clock—midnight—

before fusing their mouths together. As both of them whispered oh God, oh God, oh God, Vaughn bared his teeth against River's swollen lips and pushed through River's virginity. His prolonged growl of pleasure was eventually followed by River's, the bed springs and distant sounds of televisions blaring joined them to create a symphony all their own.

On behalf of 1001 Dark Nights,
Liz Berry and M.J. Rose would like to thank ~

Steve Berry
Doug Scofield
Kim Guidroz
Jillian Stein
InkSlinger PR
Dan Slater
Asha Hossain
Chris Graham
Pamela Jamison
Jessica Johns
Dylan Stockton
Richard Blake
BookTrib After Dark
The Dinner Party Show
and Simon Lipskar

Made in the USA
Charleston, SC
12 August 2016